My Inv

by Jaer A

MW00914925

Jaer Media Group

SCRIPT & SCRIBE
PUBLISHING

Jaer Media Group

Script & Scribe Publishing

St. Louis, Missouri

www.jaerarmsteadjones.com

SCAN ME

The Script & Scribe Publishing name and logo are trademarks of Jaer Media Group LLC.

ISBN 978-1-09837-700-7 (printed)

978-1-09837-701-4 (ebook)

Printed in the United States of America

Dedication

To my father, Gaylord X. Armstead. I thank you for your love and support throughout the years. I learned so much from you and see so much of you in me. May your soul forever rest in peace. I deeply miss you. To my wife, Shiloh Marie and my children, Camilah Selae, Lael AbriAnna, Jaelan Kyél Xzavier, and Kielan Jared. You all have helped me become the husband and father I am today. You are my treasure. To my parents, Rhonda and Melvin Jones. For opening up the doors of life through your direction and prayers. You have always been in my corner. I hope I have made you proud. To my brothers, Chris and Jevon and my sisters Karmin and Annetria, and to my extended family: I love you all and proud to be a branch in our family tree.

Acknowledgments

Many people supported this project, and I want to take time to thank you publicly. This book would not have developed without your help. Thank you for your resources, your encouragement, your work behind the scenes, your professional advice:

My Two Cents Editing: Meghan Pinson & Matthew Arkin, Kim Tolliver, Jordan Haddock, Katie Kraushaar, Kendra Day, Elizabeth Goosen, Dane Gasparovic, Sheri Wells, Stacy Camden, Rachel Lowe, Gail Tumminello, Liz Forderhase, Officer Cam McCullough, the staff and students at Hixson Middle School, Paula Juelich and Family, Randy and Sherri Rachal, The Long Family, Joel Svoboda and Family, Matt Jones, The Ewing Family, Steve Crock, Dave Cheatham and Family, Quincy Moore and Family, Richard and Charlene James, Dr. Raphael and Pastor Brenda Green, John Scates and Family, Chris and Carol Green. And to all who poured into me.

My Invisible Father

by Jaer Armstead-Jones

Scan the QR Code to view the music video for the song "Hott Heat" by Souljaristic ENT

The entire *Invisible* EP by Souljaristic ENT to be available for downloading and streaming on major streaming services.

PROLOGUE

Scan the QR Codes to read the two short stories which provide the back story for *My Invisible Father*.

"Decision of a Lifetime"

"Birth Pains"

Part 1

School Daze

"Seeking him out may have been the worst decision of my life."

~ Jayrin Foster

"So, why did I feel so good and so terrible at the same time?"

~ Kamree Covington

"I guess I knew what it felt like to walk to the gas chamber."

~ Aceson Denner

CHAPTER 1 ~ Jayrin

✱✱✱✱✱✱✱✱✱

My heart throttled in my chest, revved up like an over-the-top muscle car engine. The anxiousness, nervousness, fear, and excitement all boiled up in me at the same time.

I'd never skipped out of school before. Dymond said it was a piece of cake. Simply wait for the lunch bell to ding and run through the side door. The door alarm would be drowned out by the roaring, ringing blare of the bell and would stop as soon as the door slammed shut. Great timing was everything. The school resource officer would be forced to detangle traffic jams in the hallways, so he would ignore the doors. By the time the office staff was aware the alarm had gone off, Dymond and I would be gone with the wind. He said we'd get away scot-free.

However, I was far from convinced.

I stood in the hall and faked an in-depth conversation with Dymond while my stomach twisted in knots like a pretzel. We waited a couple of minutes for the bell to ring, but those two short minutes seemed to take hours. Then the magic happened. The blared sound signaled the freshman students to leave the lunchroom and head to fourth-hour classes. For me, 9th-grade geometry, Dymond had an elective to attend. Instead, we headed the other direction, away from hard seats and whiteboards in classrooms and outside into the chilly air.

We ran.

In no time, we arrived at Albury Park, two blocks from South City Progressional Prep, but we didn't stop running. A few blocks later I saw vehicles parked on the streets. Blue cars. Old, rusty ones. Tricked out trucks. Abandoned cars with missing tires. I was running faster than I had ever run before.

My chest started burning, and I suddenly became conscious that I ran much slower than I believed. Dymond had a whole thirty yards on me. He stopped and waited for me.

"Dang, dude, you slow as hell," Dymond said.

I felt like I was hyperventilating. Breathing hard, I choked out, "I'm not used to running for that long."

"I tell you one thing, Jayrin. If you want to do this, there may be times when you will need to run. Sometimes run for your life. So you better get used to it."

Dymond was an athlete. Tall and lean. Muscular. He ran track and played basketball in middle school. I didn't know him well then. We were familiar with each other, although we didn't hang out or consider ourselves friends. We had a few classes together. Once we entered high school, though, I sought him out. I knew about his reputation. Yeah, Dymond was bright, like me, but something else about him intrigued me. Seeking him out may have been the worst decision of my life. And that's when things went from bad to worse.

****

Sitting in the bathroom stall became almost a daily routine for me. I hated being in the cafeteria. I would gobble my food hastily and go to the restroom for some alone time. Even though nearly seventy-five freshmen sat together, eating, chatting, laughing, texting, checking out social media apps, and enjoying thirty minutes of class-free moments, I always still considered myself lonely in the midst of it.

I sat with my best friend, Kaprina. However, her other friends never attempted to befriend me. Ashamedly, I admitted to myself that though Kaprina was my bestie, I don't think I was hers. At the lunch table, she would ignore me while she engulfed herself in the space of many other girls. She was so much more popular than I was, especially once we started high school.

People said I was pretty, but my goodness, Kaprina— she was a freakin' goddess. She was gorgeous with the shape of a woman. Her banging body was the reason older boys flocked to her when school started about a month ago. Her long, dark hair and deep brown eyes matched perfectly with her caramel-toned skin.

Before long, she got snatched up by a cute boy named Kavanaugh. A junior on the football team, Kav proved to be one of the most well-known and well-liked students at Progressional. I had to confess that they appeared to be the perfect couple, but I believe Prina probably wouldn't admit it.

Soon after Kaprina and Kav got together, she started urging me to get hooked up. I didn't have any boyfriends in middle school; my mom and stepdad said I couldn't date at that young age. Once I got into high school, they said I could date, but I just couldn't go on dates. That left me confused, but I just took it as it was and tried to make the best of it.

To be honest, I wasn't comfortable with the whole idea of going out with someone. I didn't know how going out with someone was supposed to work. There was, however, a boy who I found attractive. His name was Travathian, and he was short with long, stringy dreads, a slight mustache, and dressed as if he stayed in the mall.

Someone told me he moved from Kansas City to St. Louis right before school started. Kaprina approached him one day and told him I liked him, and that sparked him to approach me in the hall. My nerves ran wild while I spoke to him, considering I had never had a boyfriend before. But Kaprina, who probably had boyfriends since she turned three, calmed me with soothing words. I'm sure I looked lame with my friend standing there while a boy was trying to talk to me.

Travathian and I started "dating" and things seemed to be going well. We would talk on the phone every night before going to bed. We texted each other whenever we could sneak a peek at our phones at school. We couldn't go anywhere together, outside of school, so we had to make the most of the time we did have in school. I began sitting with him some days at the lunch table. After two weeks, we had not kissed yet, but we did share several hugs. They made me tingle inside. I felt warm and wanted.

Eventually, he asked for a kiss. I thought the fact that he hadn't asked for one up to that point demonstrated he was patient and probably could be trusted. He didn't seem like he would try to rush into anything or pressure me into something

I didn't want. So, I conceded I should let him kiss me. Besides, I wanted to kiss him—something I'd never done to any boy.

We met after school at my locker before getting on our buses. I glanced around and hoped no one paid any attention to us.

"So, you ready for this?" Travathian asked as he slipped his backpack off his shoulder and flipped it on the floor.

"Yes, I am," I whispered. I observed that no one was aware of our actions. We were in the freshmen hallway on a busy intersection with freshmen boys and girls wrapped up in their own worlds. They were having seemingly meaningful conversations, some walking, and texting, utterly unaware of their surroundings. Others had fits while they struggled to pull bulky items from their narrow lockers. A line of sweat gradually dripped down the middle of my back.

"Here?" he replied.

"Yes," I said hesitantly while one arm held on to a book in my locker, and my other arm looked for something to do. My eyes lingered on my textbook.

"Ok." Travathian delicately touched my face trying to turn it to him. As my face slowly revolved towards his, my eyes created a life of their own. They stayed stuck to my locker for no apparent reason. I rapidly chewed the mint gum I had put in my mouth as soon as the 7th-hour bell rang. Tra tried to plant his lips right in the center of mine. I finally looked into his dark eyes, and then I swiftly shifted my face ever-so-slightly, so his smooth, soft lips landed on my right cheek instead of my lips. His lips remained there for about five seconds, and my inexperience made that the most awkward five seconds ever.

I heard the disappointment in his sigh. But his voice told a different story. "That was great." That sounded forced. He swallowed and picked up his backpack. "I better let you go so you can catch your bus. Talk to you tonight."

By this time, I sensed the entire freshman hallway had fixed their eyes on me. But as Tra disappeared, I noticed most of the students vanished as well. I experienced a quick tinge of panic shoot through me, and I quickly pulled out my backpack and threw some books into it. I didn't have time to check if they were the ones I needed. I didn't want to miss my bus.

After several more days as boyfriend and girlfriend, I finally allowed our lips to touch. Those delicate kisses had me feeling close to Travathian, but they also placed a ton of guilt on me. Like I had done something wrong, but I didn't want to stop. My mom never actually said I couldn't kiss a boy. Anyway, I couldn't get pregnant if my boyfriend gave me a peck on the cheek or the lips, for that matter. So, why did I feel so good and so terrible at the same time? I suppressed my guilty feelings and soaked in the warmth of closeness.

After a few more weeks of getting closer to Tra, I found out why he came to St. Louis in the first place. And I didn't like what I learned. So, one day before going to lunch, I asked him about it. He didn't deny it. He started to explain himself, but I immediately told him we were no longer a couple. I ran away as he grabbed my arm and yelled my name. I broke loose from his grip and bolted into the girls' bathroom, closed the stall door, and cried like a baby.

I couldn't take it anymore. These stupid girls kept at it. I held my cool even though I was red hot on the inside. So, I gawked at those girls like they were crazy and threw insults right back at them. That was usually how students handled disputes at Visionary Catholic Middle. No one ever got into a real fight.

Then Joseph Mulligan tried to add his two cents. "Hey, Mount St. Denner, can I climb up your bumpy face?"

Pimples.

Those were the only things anybody could say about my looks. Other than those craters on my face, I happened to be a decent-looking guy. I had dark blond hair and a nice tan. My family went on summer vacations every year, either somewhere in Florida or an island in the Caribbean. And we went to our condo in San Diego during winter break. I spent most of my vacation time sitting on the beach soaking up the sun.

So, when Joseph said something about my acne for the umpteenth time, I lost it.

I swung my right fist like a hammer and landed on his thin nose so swiftly that his face instantly turned from ash white to blood-red—this shocked everyone.

Including me.

The narrow hallway remained dead silent for at least ten seconds. Kids walked by looking at the scene like a car accident; they knew they shouldn't have stared, yet everyone stopped and created a traffic jam, which brought more attention to what had just happened. One girl had her mouth in the shape of a small 'O' as she fixed her gaze on me.

Joseph sat on his butt with his hand going from his face

to mid-air as he looked at his blood-drenched hand, saying, "What did you do?"

Soon, Mr. Fogerty, my science teacher, power-walked through the long corridor. Everyone parted on either side like the Red Sea. Fogerty, dressed in his usual grey khaki pants, white dress shirt, dark tie and wire-rimmed glasses, saw the massacre, and his eyes got as big as full moons.

"Girls, go retrieve some paper towels from the restroom, quickly," Fogerty pronounced. A group of like five girls scampered off to the girls' bathroom, even though it only took one person to get some freaking paper towels. And just as soon as the door closed, it opened again with the girls desperately holding out a wad of towels for Mr. Fogerty.

"What happened?" Mr. Fogerty asked sharply.

No one in the school ever wanted to snitch on anyone except when that anyone happened to be me. Never any shortage of voices who chimed in to speak my name. But no one had to say anything. They just looked at me, and Mr. Fogerty knew.

"Denner!" Mr. Fogerty yelled. "What did you do?" he asked, as he recklessly wiped up blood. Wasn't he supposed to be wearing gloves or something?

"He smashed me in the face for no reason," Joseph said, holding his head up slightly.

"Take this towel and hold it on your nose." Fogerty stood up. "Ms. Phillips, can you please walk Mr. Mulligan to the nurse's office?"

Ashley Phillips, a typical goody-two-shoes, nodded and grabbed Joseph's unoccupied arm and slowly walked him down the hallway.

"Aceson Denner, you go straight to the office this very moment. I will be there shortly."

"But I—"

"Go! Now!"

I trudged down the crowded hallway and sensed every pair of eyes in the world trailing me. The walk was long and painful, with me being the center of attention.

I opened the door to the office, and Ms. Fairbanks considered me with a disinterested glance. "Aceson. What'd you do this time?" Her words were emotionless.

"I punched Joseph in the nose. He was—" but before I could continue, she had the phone up to her ear and her finger on a button.

"Yes, sir," I heard her say. "It's Aceson. He punched another student." She paused. "Yes, sir, I will." She put the receiver down and pointed toward the principal's office. "He said to go in. No need to knock."

I guess I knew what it felt like to walk to the gas chamber. I was walking to my own death as I entered Dr. Hamilton's office. As soon as I sat down, Mr. Fogerty stammered into the office. "Dr. Hamilton, apparently Mr. Denner here struck Joseph Mulligan for no reason." I dropped my head in disgust and noticed drops of blood on my white polo and tan khaki pants.

"Did you get statements?" Dr. Hamilton asked Mr. Fogerty.

This time I interrupted. I lifted my head and said sadly, "No need for statements. I hit Joseph because he said something about my face."

Mr. Hamilton's lips twitched. He blew out a long,

exhausting breath. Then he picked up the phone. "I guess we'll have to call your father."

He started dialing. Geez, did he memorize my father's cell number? Man, I was in deep doo-doo.

"Yes, James, this is Ryan Hamilton at VCM. How are you?" Is he on a first-name basis with my father? What the heck! I know he called my father many times for all the trouble I caused, but I was never in the room when he did. "Well, unfortunately, James, I'm calling to give you some bad news. Again. But this is more severe than his usual antics."

I gulped for air, feeling like I was having an asthmatic attack. And I didn't have asthma. I was in no shape to be running at such a high speed in such a short burst. Dymond was breathing easily. *Breathe through your nose*, he had told me. Better chance for oxygen to get into your lungs. I tried it, and I felt like I was going to pass out.

"You gotta ditch that old raggedy backpack," Dymond said, noticing my sweaty exhaustion. "It's holding you down." I tried to speak between my wheezing, but nothing came out.

"Why you wearing it anyway?" he asked.

I found the strength to eek something out of my panting mouth. "For school. You know, books and stuff."

Dymond *humphed*.

I collapsed on a rickety porch, where Dymond had already planted himself. "Why are we sitting here?" I asked.

"This is our spot."

"This is only a couple blocks from my house," I said. The block was a one-way street, like most streets in the area.

"Yeah, is that a problem?" Dymond responded.

"No. It's not a problem."

"Okay. Stay here. I'll be right back." Dymond hopped off the steps and walked around the side of the house.

The house was white but dingy and stained. The front porch was made of broken concrete with wooden steps, and the steps were missing nails in some places and had nails sticking up and out in others. There were holes in the steps apparently where the handrail must've been. The grass in the front yard was dead, brown with patches of grass missing.

Looked like a dirty boy with a horrible haircut. I looked up and down the street. Many of the houses resembled this one; they also looked like the houses on my block. Many homes were boarded up and drenched with graffiti.

A light breeze gave me a slight chill from the sweat on my forehead and a somewhat damp undershirt. It was a cloudy day, which made it feel cooler than it was. It was the end of September and barely fall. Leaves were still full in many trees, and they rustled while blowing in the wind. And I couldn't stop asking myself if this was a good idea. Was this really what I wanted to do?

Dymond came back, and I jumped out of my thoughts. He sat on the step above me, and his hand magically appeared to my right with bags of marijuana. His gloved hand presented it to me, and I timidly reached out to grab one of the bags. "No, take them all," he insisted.

"Oh," I said in a slightly disappointed voice. "I thought the others were yours."

He shook his head. "No, I already got mine. This here is your first batch. All of it."

"Thanks," I said, with little gratitude.

"Now, let me show you where we keep these."

We walked to the side of the house and opened up the dryer vent cover. "The bags go in here," Dymond said.

I had a quizzical look on my face. "In the dryer vent? Won't they blow away or something?"

"No, this is a fake. Monae's real dryer is on the other side of the house. This one is just to keep the dope. She puts them in here every day just before we get here. You keep a few bags with you, and when you sell some, you come back and get a few more for the next sales. Now let me show you where we put the money."

We walked back to the front of the house. "The money goes here in the mail slot." The mail slot was on the front door, where mail was dropped inside. "As a junior member, you get three dollars for every dime bag you sell and one dollar for every nickel bag."

I quickly did the math in my head. "So, I get thirty percent for every dime bag and twenty percent for every nickel bag?" It was a question, but I knew I was correct. "Why the difference?"

"The more you sell, the more you make. You keep your cut from each sale; the rest you put in the mail slot." Over the past couple of weeks, Dymond schooled me on selling weed but had not discussed the money aspect in this much depth.

A few cars had passed by as we intently looked to see if they were going to stop or not. Finally, one did stop and flashed the headlights even though it was still high noon on an overcast day. It was a blue Chevy Equinox. Looked like a 2016. "Okay, this is one of my regular customers, but no matter if they are regulars or first-timers, the routine stays the same," Dymond said. "We already talked about how to make the exchange, so watch me in action because you may be up next."

I watched Dymond cross the street with a light jog, looking both ways as he crossed. His last few steps before arriving at the car displayed carefulness with slow, gentle strides. He once again peered up and down the street. Because we were on a one-way street, the driver's side window was on the sidewalk side of the road. The window glided down. Dymond carefully examined inside the car and swiveled his head around once more before sticking his hand through the window, and I noticed what appeared to be him shaking hands with the man in the car. Dymond slid his arm out of the car, turned, and walked behind the vehicle into the street.

The car took off, and Dymond trotted back to the porch and sat next to me. The whole thing took about a minute.

"As easy as that, bruh. Can you handle it?"

Instantly, I felt queasy. Even though there weren't any cars coming down the street, I knew that I could be the one to make the next sale as soon as one stopped. I was not looking forward to it. I felt like I would mess up or get robbed or get shot. I guess everyone had a first time, and if you made it through the first one, you'd get a second one. And before you knew it, you became a real pro at it. But I felt like I was never going to get to that point. "Yeah, I'm ready," I said, with fake confidence.

A few moments later, my time had come. A dope-looking, white sports car stopped across the street and blinked its lights twice—the signal for someone looking to buy. I looked at Dymond as I hesitantly stood up. "This is not one of your regulars?" I asked, hoping he would say yes.

His eyes bore into mine, and I could tell he knew I was afraid. "Bruh, you think you got the balls for this?"

I nodded my head as I attempted to walk down the brittle wooden steps of the dilapidated house without falling and breaking my neck. Partly because I was trying to avoid stepping on a rusty nail, partially because the steps were shaking, and so was I.

I walked to the street, looked both ways, then fake-jogged over to the car. I was so scared, I thought I was going to poop my pants. It was a nice-looking car. A Mazda CX-5. Not too expensive, but new and nice. Just for a second, I forgot what I was supposed to do. Then the tinted window scrolled down. Inside was a lady—a young white lady in a nice business suit. Then, for some reason, my fear and anxiousness left. I looked at her like she was a lost kitten. She looked at me like I was a lost puppy. I stood there waiting for her to do something. She sat there waiting for me to do something.

"Two dime bags," she said, with a soft, yet demanding voice.

I clumsily stuck my hand inside the car, and she slipped a bill in my hand. I saw that it was a twenty, then I slid my hands in my sleeves and pulled out two dime bags. I gave them to her and looked intently into her eyes. Without flinching, she put the car in drive and took off with my arm still partially inside. I jumped back quickly, hoping she wouldn't roll over my foot. I stood there, watching the car speed down the street.

Paralyzed, I heard Dymond loudly whisper my name. "Jayrin!" My gaze remained on the white car as it disappeared in the daylight. "Jayrin!" I heard him again, and I jerked myself back to reality. I jogged back over to the other side of the street and sat down on the dusty steps.

"You need to keep your head on a swivel," Dymond barked. "Before you put your hand in a car, you should look inside the car to make sure you don't see any weapons and be sure you see the customer's hands. Then you must be aware of your surroundings to make sure no one else is around or looking. Check for hands and weapons again. You must do that every time. Didn't we talk about this?"

"Yeah, we did, but I just... I guess I just forgot," I said sheepishly. "And besides, it was just a little white lady."

Dymond's face quickly turned into a serious meme.

"I don't care if it was a ninety-year-old grandma with angel wings; it's the same routine every time," he said sternly. "You take no one for granted because if you mess up, you might as well be dead."

After a couple of minutes, I heard the bathroom door squeak open, and I tried to hide my sniffles, but they kept leaking out. Suddenly a voice my ears recognized stopped my tears in their tracks. "Kamree."

"Prina?" I asked with a little certainty.

"Girl, what you doing in here crying?"

I opened the door with as little squeaking as possible, trying to make sure no one else was out there. "I just broke up with Tra," I whispered.

"Broke up?" Kaprina asked, way too loudly. "Y'all didn't even date but a few weeks. That don't qualify for breaking up. And, if you, so-called, broke up with him, why are you the one in here crying?"

"Because I thought I had finally found someone I could be with. My first boyfriend. I thought Tra was the one."

Kaprina grunted a chuckle. "The one? The one? How you ever gonna find the one if you are a stuck-up lil church girl from the hood? Besides, you way too young to be trying to find the one." My head nodded slightly, even though I didn't want to agree with her.

"Why do you think I have at least two boyfriends every year? Cause niggas ain't no good, so I use them up till I don't need them no more. Take me to parties, take me to the mall," her head bouncing from side to side as she was running down her list, "buy me stuff, and then maybe I give them a few kisses or whatever. It's wrong to be looking for Mr. Right. He'll always be Mr. Wrong until he put a ring on it. And even then..." her voice trailed off.

Suddenly, I realized Kaprina had eased in the stall with me and how weird that appeared. She didn't seem to care. "So why did you break up with him?"

My timid feet tried to walk out of the stall casually, but Prina stood in my way. "I was told why he left Kansas City. He was in juvenile, and his mother wanted him to come here and live with his cousin and aunt to escape his environment."

"To St. Louis? To escape his environment?" Kaprina blurted sarcastically.

"Yeah. He needed to leave and start over."

"What did he go to juvie for?"

"Assault."

"So he had a fight? That doesn't make him all bad."

"He beat up a girl. Put her in the hospital."

Kaprina stood silent as her eyes shot up in wonderment. That gave me time to quickly creep out of the stall. I walked over to the sink and turned the water on. "Oh! Yeah, that's a perfect reason to want to cancel dude. Any nigga that hits a girl is a straight-up punk. Kam, you did right."

"Yeah, but now I'm scared," I said slowly.

"Scared of what?"

I gave Prina a 'duh' look.

"Oh. Scared he might come after you?" Prina said in the form of a question that also sounded like a statement. Her eyes darted from me to the large rectangular mirror. However, I sensed her continuing to look at my reflection. "How that fool get in a school like this anyway?"

"Like everybody else, he must have taken the test, passed it, and then was selected in the lottery. There were no questions on the application asking if you'd ever been in juvie or committed a crime."

"Yeah, I guess so, but they had to ask about his previous school records. They had to know he got bounced."

"The thing is, he wasn't kicked out. Tra assaulted the girl a few days after the school year was over. He spent about a month locked up over the summer, but his school was probably not informed about it. His educational records were obviously fine."

Someone came into the bathroom, and I put water in my hands and splashed my face.

"How did you get all this information?" Prina inquired, completely ignoring another girl standing next to us. She received another 'duh' stare from me. She turned to the girl who was fingering her hair, looking at her reflection. "Don't you got somewhere to go? Shouldn't you be in class or something?" Prina asked harshly.

The girl, whose name was Lexiah, looked at Prina like she was crazy. "Shouldn't you be in class?" Lexiah asked with a neck-rolling attitude.

"Oh no, missy. You don't come at me like that. Obviously, you don't recognize who I am."

"I don't need to recognize who you are to kick your—"

I quickly stepped in between them and held Prina back as I saw them squaring up. "Okay, no need to be fighting for nothing. We all need to leave and go to class."

"Yeah, you lucky your little girlfriend saved yo' little, fat butt," Lexiah said.

"Well, your man likes my fat butt," Prina shot back.

"That's because he used to be your man. Then I took him from you. So, he obviously likes mine better." Lexiah gave her the middle finger, turned, and walked toward the door.

Again, I had to hold Prina back as she started breathing like a wild bull. Lexiah began walking out while Prina called her a B. And she couldn't let the girl leave in peace. "Next time you interrupt my conversation, Imma pull your lil cheap weave off your nappy head and fake lashes off your face, trick!"

I turned to Prina, dumbfounded. "Girl, don't you wear a weave and fake lashes, too?"

"Yeah, but mine make me look gorgeous. That skank look like a tarantula with horsehair."

With that, I busted out laughing. In the bathroom. With my best friend, Kaprina.

✱✱✱✱✱✱✱✱✱

Suspended for five days. All next week. I knew my father's anger was boiling over even though he didn't speak to me the entire twenty-minute drive home. That made it worse. The silence was deafening in my head. I kept waiting for him to yell at me or something, but it never happened. It was as if he was more interested in the talk radio voices painstakingly coming through the speakers than talking to me about the incident.

When we got home, I anticipated an eruption as soon as I dropped my backpack on the floor—still nothing. The silence killed me softly, for sure.

He went to the kitchen and quickly returned with a water bottle in his hand. I stood in the foyer, waiting for him to say something. Finally, he did.

"I'm going back to work." Then he turned and walked out the door and shut it behind him.

That was it? That was all he had to say? *'I'm going back to work.'* What in the world was going on with him? Then I realized what he was doing. He wanted me to be so afraid until he came home—so worried thinking about what he was going to do to me. And his plan worked.

My stomach started hurting. I ran upstairs to my bathroom and sat on the toilet. Then I got up and put my face over it. Didn't know which end to expect the projectile to come from, but I felt as sick as a cat who just ate a diseased rat. I was light-headed and dizzy. My breathing was rapid and heavy. My skin warm and moist. I believed I was going to pass out. I had to get a hold of myself.

I thought back to what the counselors at school talked to us about. Mindfulness or something. I calmed down and took deep breaths. My breathing and heart rate slowed down. I sat next to the pearly white toilet and thought about all the times I had gotten in trouble recently. Stupid stuff. Talking back to the teacher. Throwing spitballs. Calling girls names, but this was the first time something like this had happened.

I'd never actually hit someone. Man, did I break Joseph's nose? Did he go to the hospital? That would be terrible. Would his parents press charges against me? Oh my God! What did I do?

My heart raced against my breaths to see which could go the fastest. I cried like a baby. A tumultuous thunderstorm that I couldn't stop. A tsunami rushed down my face, and snot seeped down to my lips. Eventually, I calmed down, washed my face with cold water, looked in the mirror, and reflected on my miserable life. I had to do better.

I went back to my room and laid on the bed. I cried myself to sleep.

I woke up to a damp pillow and dried snot above my lip. I went back to the bathroom and looked at myself in the mirror again. I could barely stare for more than a second because I was so ashamed. Why was I like this? Why did I do foolish things all the time? Why did I keep getting myself into messes I couldn't clean up?

I expected my father to come home a little earlier than usual because he seemed to always do so on Fridays. Typical for him would be about six-thirty, but Fridays, he would arrive home around five-thirty. I watched the clock like a hawk. Five-twenty, five-forty-five, six o'clock came and went. I heard when you stared at the clock, time goes by slower. I studied everything besides the clock. The wall with posters. The blank wall. The hardwood floor. Six-thirty came and went.

I sat in total silence, reluctant to turn the television on because I wanted to be sure to hear when my father came into the house. My mom had arrived home; however, she didn't come to my room to say anything to me. She didn't even say hi or let me know she was home. My dad must have called and told her the great news.

Mom eventually yelled for me to come down for dinner, but I told her I didn't feel good. She left me alone. She knew what I really meant.

Then, at 6:52, the door alarm chimed, indicating someone had opened a door. My father arrived. I waited for him to come up to my room and curse me out or something. Again, nothing. At 7:15, I decided to brave the world and go downstairs to the kitchen to eat. Before I got there, I heard my parents arguing. I was certain they were arguing about me, so I sat on the carpeted steps and listened.

"I don't think he should stay here by himself all week," my mom said.

"Well, I can't be here for the whole week. Too much work to do."

"James, you own the freakin' company. You can take off whenever you want."

"Well, it's not that easy. I have appointments already set."

"That's why you hired associates. Can't Sydney or Michael handle your stupid appointments? At least some of them, so you can be home for a little while?"

"They have their own meetings to attend."

"Well, there has to be room for emergencies, James. If Aceson was in the hospital, would you put your appointments ahead of your son?"

"But he's not in the hospital, Trista," my dad said slowly and sternly. It sounded like he was extremely frustrated with my mom. "I don't understand why you think he can't stay home by himself. My God, the boy is fourteen years old. He's not a baby. He's stayed by himself before."

"Yeah, but not for a whole week? We can't trust he will make the right choices all week." Mom tried to whisper, but I clearly picked up what she said. And she was probably right. I stood and quietly headed back up the stairs to my room. As I said, I didn't feel good.

✱✱✱✱✱✱✱✱✱

I had never seen so much money in my life. Each day over the past week had been about the same. Skip out on school around lunchtime. Sit on the steps of this old ugly house, sell weed. Go home around six o'clock, eat something and then hit the spot and sell again till late at night, drop money in the house, and go home with at least one hundred dollars, and on the weekends, maybe close to two hundred and fifty. I asked Dymond if it was always like that. Once I did this for a while, he said I would start getting a bigger cut, taking home more money. He said he sometimes pulled about fifteen hundred dollars a week.

"Yeah, eventually you'll get your regular customers. You'll be getting burner phones so you can set appointments with them and know when to look for them on a daily. You have to always remember never to use your personal cell phone for any of this. Don't bring it to our spot."

"Well, you don't have to worry about that," I said.

"What you mean?"

"I don't have a cell phone."

"What? Man, who ain't got no cell phone?"

"Not me. My mom can't afford one. Said maybe when I turn sixteen."

"Dude, that's messed up." Dymond spat in the dead grass. "Don't worry, you'll be able to buy your own phone pretty soon."

"How? I'm underage."

"Don't worry about it. Monae," he pointed his head toward the house where we were sitting, "she hooks us up with everything we need."

The moon was a ginormous, bright, white lamp in the sky and provided the only light on the damp, dark block. "Yeah, I meant to ask about her. Is she like the leader or something? We giving her all the money, she must be."

"Monae? Nah, you'll never meet the top dog. But she don't keep all that money. She just one of the money bags. Collect the money and take it where it needs to go. But that ain't our business. We just gotta make sure to always get her the cut from our sales, and she takes it from there."

Dymond picked up a rock from the broken concrete steps. He examined it and threw it in the yard.

"Well, I guess that's cool," I said, "as long as we get paid, I guess it don't matter."

"So, you're doing this for the money?"

"Man, my mom is struggling to take care of me, my brother, and my sister. I'm tired of living like this. Of course, I'm doing this for the money. Ain't that what everybody doing it for?"

"Yeah, but it seems like your heart ain't in it. You a good kid. I mean, what flipped you? You used to be all about the books. You smart. Is this street life really for you?"

A rusty green Honda Accord sputtered down the street. It didn't stop.

"Cause I'm smart? You smart, too. We all supposed to be smart up in that school," I said.

Being accepted into South City Progressional Prep was considered a privilege and a big deal for us poor kids on the south side of town. We were at the top of our classes in middle school, and some of our teachers recommended we sign up for the lottery to Pro Prep, as it was known. They believed if we got out of the city public schools and into a better environment, we would have a better chance to focus on school, graduate, go to college, and do something good with our lives. But what they failed to realize is that no matter where you went, a prep school in the city or a private school in the suburbs, there was no escaping trouble. There were always weeds growing among the pretty flowers.

"Yeah, but there's different types of smart: book-smart, street-smart, and that's the difference between me and you. We both may be book-smart, but only one of us is street-smart. You ain't got no idea how to run these streets. But you could probably make it in any school."

I blew into my hands, then frantically rubbed them together, trying to find heated friction for my frigid fingers. As it got later, the temperature had dropped. Dymond wore gloves, but I struggled with my bare hands. "School's boring. I could earn any grades I want to," I said. "Classes aren't a challenge for me, but I'd rather be doing something else more exhilarating."

"More what?"

"Exhilarating. Invigorating."

"Man, I don't know what the hell you talkin' about."

"Something more exciting. Like being out here on the block. Making cash."

"I feel ya, bruh. Gotta make that money, but didn't you ever think about going to college?"

"I mean, I thought about it, but, as I said, I'm bored with school. As soon as I turn sixteen, I'm done. Peace out, deuces," I said while holding up two fingers.

"You don't think college would be a challenge? You said

you needed to be challenged, right?"

"Well, yeah, but..." Blue Chevy Impala. Stops and flashes headlights.

"This one's me," Dymond said. "One of my regulars." He staggered off the steps and jogged to the curb. He looked both ways, and so did I. I made sure no one hid in the creases waiting in the cut to jump him. I had to be sure no police cars rolled up. He crossed the street and made the transaction in no time. Very smooth.

"Now, what was you saying?" Dymond asked after sliding money inside the mail slot.

"Well, by the time I turn eighteen, I'm hoping to be deep in the game, high up on the ladder, looking down on all these runners like they doing us now—weed, heroin, meth. I want to sell it all. I won't have time for college. I'm going to be posted up on the block, making moves like a power forward."

"Nigga, please! Talking like you understand basketball. You ain't no athlete, you a mathlete." Dymond laughed hard, losing his balance slightly, nearly falling off the step.

Dymond was a great athlete. He won Amateur Athletic Union medals for track and played Junior Football League wide receiver. He was right; I never participated in any sports except in P.E. class, and I was horrible at all sports in gym class— always picked last in everything.

"Naw, I'm all about the trap now," I said, referring to the neighborhood used as an operation to sell drugs. "I'm all about getting that bread, getting that cheese."

"They putting that cheese in the trap 'cause they don't want us to escape," Dymond said. I looked at him with a furrowed forehead. He shook his head. "They invest money into the hood with dope and guns, knowing that we gonna go after it like rats going after cheese, and once we get a taste, we won't be able to leave. That's why they call it the trap. A rat trap. For hood rats like me. But you...you got a mind that could take you out of here, bro."

"Are you telling me I should stop slangin?"

"I'm telling you this life ain't for you."

"What makes you such an expert on what I should do with my life?"

"Jay, you have no idea what it's like out here. You gotta be all in, or it will do you in. You either kill or be killed. This ain't no game, homie. I've been doing this since 7th grade. I was practically born in the game."

The cold wind chewed through my black hoodie and jeans. The chill squeezed my body, and I started shaking like a leaf.

"Monae. She my brother's girlfriend. You heard of my brother?"

I nod. Dymond's brother Dynastie was the biggest drug dealer in the hood. "Yeah, I remember him. Can't help but know who he is. How long he locked up for anyway?"

"He got ten years, but he might be out in six or seven."

"And then he'll be right back on the block?"

"All we do is hustle. It started with my pops and my uncles. We gotta uphold the family business," Dymond said, with a sly grin showing the gold grill glistening in his mouth.

"So your father out here pushing too?"

"Man, my father got murdered about five, six years ago."

"Got shot?"

"Yep. Not sure if some fool robbed him for his dope and

money or another dealer just wanted to off him. Or it could've been one of his little soldiers trying to be on top."

"Wow, that's cold."

"Yeah, once you blow up so big, anybody would be gunning for the number one spot. Sometimes you gotta do somebody cause they trying to take over your block."

"So, your dad was the man, huh? But if he's dead, how do you not know who's the top dog now."

"I know who's the top dog on the block. But it's a chain of cats that go from our hood all the way to them bad dudes in Mexico, South America, Canada, and even in Asia, bro. They get the dope into the states, and mules drive down the pipeline to New Orleans, San Antonio, and up to Detroit and Chicago and transport the dope here. The big dogs buy it up, give it to the senior runners, and the senior runners give it to street soldiers to sell on the street. It's complicated because it's a business, man."

"Dang, how you know all this?"

"Pops hipped Dynastie, and once pops died, Dynastie put me on game."

"You miss your father?"

"I don't remember much about him. I was much younger when he was around. And when he was around, he wasn't really around. You know what I mean?"

"Actually, I don't. I ain't got no father. Or at least I ain't never met him. That nigga don't want nothing to do with me. I mean, as far as I'm concerned, he's just as dead as your pops."

Every time I asked my mom about my father, she acted as if she didn't want to talk about him. Almost like he didn't exist. So, for me, he didn't. I think at seven or eight years old; I remember asking her if she could call him so he could come see me.

She gave me some lame excuse, like he got his phone number changed or he moved, and she couldn't make contact with him. A few years later, I asked again. And again, nothing. Finally, because she probably got tired of me asking, she came clean and told me the truth. At least, I think it was the truth.

****

"Jay. Come into my room. I need to talk to you about something."

I walked into her room, shaky for some reason. Mom always had these little talks with me about stuff, but I had a bad feeling about this one.

"Well, honey." She swallowed hard. I wondered if her heart was beating as fast as mine. "I'm quite aware you've been wondering and inquiring about your father. You're twelve years old, and I'm quite certain now is the time you knew the truth."

My insides did somersaults as I flipped from extremely nervous to excessively frightened. She opened her mouth, and nothing came out. Then seconds later, she began again. "I did send him a letter explaining that you wanted to meet him and that it would be good for you to have a father in your life. I even called him, and he told me—"

"You said you couldn't get in touch with him," I interrupted. "Mama, you lied to me?"

"I'm sorry, Son. I did lie, only to protect you."

"Protect me from what?" I demanded, probably a little too sternly. But I felt like I could get away with it seeing how sorrowful my mom looked.

"Well, sweetie, the fact is he doesn't want to meet you."

My mom paused, expecting a reaction from me, but I didn't move. I didn't change my facial expression one bit. I sat still as a statue.

"I know this may be disappointing to hear, but I want you to understand that it'll be okay. I will always be here for you. You are truly loved."

I twisted my face in disappointment and hurt, and I swallowed a lump of spit that rolled down my throat like a lubricated bowling ball. "But my father doesn't want to meet me. He doesn't want me. What did I do for him not to want me?" I held every tear that wanted to escape the depths of my eyes, determined not to let the devastation control my emotions.

"You have done absolutely nothing to make him be this way, Son." She began sniffling, trying desperately to finish making her point. "He didn't want a child from the beginning. He wanted nothing to do with you even before you were born."

"What the hell does that mean?" I felt way too liberal with my words. I'm surprised my mom didn't slap the taste out of my mouth. "He didn't want nothing to do with me before I was born?"

"Well, yes, but it's complicated."

I began shaking my head furiously, a hot rage continually building up. "Complicated. What does that mean?" I asked explosively.

A long, deafening silence followed.

Finally, my mother spoke again. "Well, he didn't think that I was going to keep you."

In the span of thirty seconds, I traveled from totally angry to completely confused. Shaking my head again, all I could say was, "He didn't think you were going to keep me?"

CHAPTER 8 ~ Kamree

✲✲✲✲✲✲✲✲

On Monday morning, a chattering and screaming buzz filled the hallway. There weren't too many fights at South City Pro Prep, so I had a hard time believing a blood-drenched brawl fueled the source of the excitement. No one showed signs of getting to class. Girls were crying. Like all-out boo-hoo crying. What in the world had happened? Kaprina lingered in the gathering. She wasn't sobbing but appeared distressed.

"Girl, what is going on?" I inquired.

"You didn't hear?" she returned in disbelief.

"Hear what?"

"Erique!"

"Erique Timmons?"

"Yes, girl."

"What?"

"Did you hear about the boy who got shot in a car last night on Virginia?"

"Yeah, it was on TV. The twelfth kid killed in the city since the beginning of summer. They didn't release a name."

"It was Erique."

"What makes you so sure it was Erique?"

"His sister posted it on Snapchat this morning."

My mouth gaped open. My throat paralyzed shut. A cry bubbled in my depths, but my eyes felt frozen. I couldn't move. Erique, the seventeen-year-old star of the basketball squad, seemed to be liked by everyone who knew him, and he appeared to be a cool boy. He apparently transferred last year from Webster Groves High School, one of the best basketball schools in the area.

I wouldn't consider him cute, but he always dressed nice, and because of his athletic status, many girls threw themselves at him from what I saw. However, he didn't let his athletic prowess go to his head; he wasn't egotistical. He would always treat people right, and I never knew him to be in trouble at school. I hadn't seen him play basketball yet, because the season hadn't started, but I heard he had a half dozen scholarship offers.

Could it have been a mistake? An innocent bystander? This made my blood boil. Too many kids were dying to all the violence in our city. I was fed up with it.

"Why would anyone kill Erique?"

"Not sure, but rumors are going around saying he sold drugs," Prina said.

"I don't believe it," I said.

"Girl, you didn't even know him like that."

"Yeah, but he didn't carry himself like that."

"We can't look at nobody and tell if they selling or using or nothing. Looks can be deceiving. Yeah, he was popular and always seemed to do the right thing at school. Everybody assumed he was a decent kid. All the while, he could have been hiding the fact that he was a drug dealer."

"Yeah, I guess it's possible," I said. "You said he got shot in a car. He had a car? Didn't he take the bus to school?"

"Yeah, he did, but the car happened to be a silver Lexus. His stupid sister took a picture of the car, showing all the bullet holes and everything? Posted it on Snapchat. She said the car belonged to him. He didn't drive to school probably because people would wonder."

I began shaking my head. "I am so tired of this."

"So tired of what?" chimed in another voice.

My heart jumped out of my chest. "Jayrin, you scared me. I didn't notice you behind me."

"I noticed behind you. And you look good back there."

Jayrin was a friend. He attended the same middle school where Prina and I went. I'm so happy we all ended up at the same high school together. He was kind of cute with gorgeous, light brown eyes, but skinny and always wore bummy clothes. Cute boys not having hip clothes were rare, but Jayrin was one of them. Kids at our school weren't rich, but Jayrin was super poor.

He never did anything which required money; no dances, no games, he didn't hang out with us at McDonald's after school. Still, Jayrin had a likable personality. He always had something corny to say to me, though. Always talking like he wanted to get with me. I don't think he ever had a girlfriend, but I never gave him a chance despite his attempts. I had not been interested in boys until high school. I was too busy trying to excel in my grades, and I didn't want added stress of keeping up with boys.

"Jayrin, this is a serious situation. Did you hear what happened to Erique?" I asked.

Prina walked away to students by a water fountain.

"Nope. What happened?"

"He got shot and killed last night. You didn't see on the TV news a kid got shot on Virginia Street?"

Jayrin displayed a perplexed glare. "I don't watch the news. Who watches the news?"

"I watch the news."

"That's lame."

Prina came and grabbed my arm, then pulled me away from Jayrin. Good thing she did because I was about to let him have it.

"What, Prina?"

"Yo, we don't have to go to class," she said excitedly. "The school's bringing in a bunch of counselors to the cafeteria to talk to us if we are having emotional issues dealing with Erique's death."

"We weren't even acquainted with him that well."

"You said you are tired of this, and now you have an opportunity to express your feelings. Get them out to help you deal with all of this going on. Plus, no class!"

"Yeah, but what use will that be?"

Jayrin walked over to us. "What's going on now?" he asked.

"Prina said we could skip classes to talk with some counselors about Erique's death."

"Really? You going?"

"No, I'm not going," I said.

"Why not?"

"She's too righteous to be doing something just to skip class," Prina shot back.

"Tell me, Prina, what is skipping class going to solve?"

"Kam, you can't think you'll always solve everything. You forever trying to save the world, but this is real life, not some book you read where the main character always wins in the end."

I regarded Prina. Amazingly, I considered her my best friend, even though she sometimes said the stupidest things.

"I'm not trying to save the world," I retorted, "but I wish we could do something about this stuff happening in this city. All these carjackings. Rolling gun battles. All these killings. Kids our age murdered every week. Some are younger than us.

"If a White cop killed Erique, people would be marching in the streets, protesting, rioting, looting; that's what we do in this stupid city. Why are we not up in arms when some Black person kills another Black person? Why don't people get angry at that?"

"What makes you so sure somebody Black murdered Erique?" Jayrin asked ever so politely.

"Yeah, how you know that?" Prina repeated, not as nicely.

I rolled my eyes at them. "I don't know," I said with an attitude, "but I know," I uttered with certainty.

"Well, you do understand White people kill other White people too? It's not just about Black-on-Black crime."

"I don't need your statistics about White-on-White crime. Because that has nothing to do with me. White-on-White crime won't kill my little brother. White-on-White crime won't kill you, Jayrin, or you, Prina. And White-on-White crime didn't kill Erique. So, don't come to me talking about White folks kill White folks too!"

"You mad, bro? What, you want us to start a riot? You want us to burn some buildings to demonstrate that we care?" Jayrin responded, a little too enthusiastically.

"Again, if a White police officer did this, people would run to reveal their frustration. But when we kill our own, we organize peaceful marches and prayer vigils."

"I thought you believed in peace. And don't you think prayer changes things? You've said that before," Prina preached to me.

"I do, but prayer without real action is just dead words floating in the air. We need to be mad at this murderous spirit running crazy in our community. We have to fight this thing. Instead, we sit around and say another dead Black boy, and of course, right after that, another one will be killed. I'm so sick and tired of this sick cycle."

"Girl, you ain't no political activist. Why you always trying to find the answer to everything? Always gotta be right. I mean, we understand Black lives matter, but you doing too much with the whole 'if it was a White cop' thing."

"What are you talking about?"

"Do you support Black Lives Matter or not? Or are you about Blue Lives Matter?" Prina asked.

"Can I not support both if I believe in both?"

"Girl, of course not. That don't make no sense. You so unorthodox," Prina said.

"So can a police officer support Black Lives Matter?" I asked. Prina paused and thought for a moment. "What about Black police officers?" I added.

She looked at me like a light bulb had been switched on in her head. She pursed her lips, but nothing came out.

"It's complicated, huh?"

"Yeah, but it's not that complicated to realize that Black people are murdered by White cops too much."

"So you think a White cop riddled Erique's car with bullets with him inside?"

"Not really," she said, "but the cop killings just won't stop. No mater what, they keep happening."

"But this ain't that," I responded.

Then I turned and walked to my first-hour class.

CHAPTER 9 ~ Aceson

✱✱✱✱✱✱✱✱

Day one of my suspension? A success! For seven hours, I ate and played Call of Duty: Black Ops. I should get suspended more often. I didn't even take off my pajamas. Didn't brush my teeth. Didn't wash my face. Awesome!

Then the home alarm system triggered. I nearly pooped my pants when the blaring siren screamed. I dropped the game controller, and I didn't move. I couldn't move. I was petrified. Someone had broken into our house, and I had on my Buzz Lightyear pajamas. Crap. Not only was I scared, but I was also embarrassed.

Suddenly, the beeps of the keypad allowed me to realize someone had turned the alarm off. My tight butt cheeks loosened up, and I figured unless a burglar knew our passcode, my father had come home to check on me.

My father confirmed my suspicions when his deep radio voice yelled upstairs. "Ace!"

"Yeah." His heavy footsteps ascended the steps.

He came in and peeped at the controller on the floor and glanced at my television. "So, what are you doing? Playing video games?"

"Well, I mean, yeah. What else am I supposed to do?"

"I don't know, read a book or something," he said as he sat on my bed next to me.

I chuckled, and my dad's fiery blue eyes pierced my dark, jittery pupils. "Oh, you were serious?"

"Yes, I was, and that's part of your problem, Ace. You are not taking things seriously enough. The same things you did in elementary school, you are still doing in middle school. You've done nothing to convince us you'll stop doing those things next year in high school. Your mother and I tried to let you grow up at your own pace, but your actions don't show progression.

"You keep doing stupid stuff, bullying people, acting a fool in class. The one good thing you got going for you right now is you bring home good grades. But other than that, you are good for nothing, and you need to realize when you do foolish things, other people are affected too!"

I frowned because I felt terrible. After all, I did so much dumb stuff, and I felt bad because my dad said I was good for nothing.

"Like, this. Taking off work to come home to check in on you."

"You don't need to check in on me. I can stay home by myself." My mind quickly went back to the whistling siren and what I would have done if it really were an intruder. "And it's your lunchtime anyway." I also wanted to say, and *you own the freakin' company, you can leave anytime you want to*, but I thought better of it.

"It doesn't matter if I'm at lunch or not, but when your ways at school start dictating how we live and work, your behaviors need to change." My dad's hand searched my bed until it found the remote control. He clicked the TV off. "The nonsense has to stop. Hopefully, this out-of-school suspension will serve as a wake-up call for you to get your act together." He paused, seemingly waiting for me to say something. I said nothing. "When will you get it together?"

I shrugged my shoulders. He shook his head.

"You moved from bad-mouthing and bullying people to punching kids in the face. If I were that kid's father, I'd tell him to hit you with a sucker punch the next time he sees you." That statement sucker punched me in my gut. "What's the deal?"

"Not sure. Bored, I guess. Sucks being alone every day. I have no friends at school. I have no one here at home. I've been asking for a brother forever."

"We've talked about this before. You understand why you have no siblings, but that should be no excuse for your behavior."

When I was about ten years old, my mom and dad sat me down and talked with me. One of the strangest conversations ever.

****

"We're aware you want a brother or sister; however, this is more complicated than that," my mom said.

"What does that even mean?" I snapped.

"It means you wouldn't understand," my dad chimed in.

"I wish you would stop treating me like a stupid kid."

"We don't think you're stupid, honey," my mom said. "You're so young. This is a grown-up situation, and we had to make adult decisions. So you don't need to know."

"You've been telling me this for years. I think I can handle it just fine if you just told me the truth."

My mom studied Dad. He folded his hands, put them on the kitchen table, and glared at me, then at my mom. "Maybe we should tell him, Trista."

My mom swallowed hard. "I don't think it's a good idea, but if you feel like we should, you tell him. However, I think it will be a mistake."

✱✱✱✱✱✱✱✱✱✱

When we were at the spot after ditching school, I wanted to ask about Erique, but the more I thought about it, the more spooked I became. I realized that I could be in the same situation that Erique ended up in. So, I hesitated to talk to Dymond about it. He'd continue to think I wasn't cut out for this.

When I went back to the porch later that I night, I decided to bring it up. "So, did you hear about that dude, Erique?" I interrogated Dymond as we sat on Monae's front porch. He peeked at me and slowly turned his head up the block. The sky echoed smoky darkness, which diminished the ability to see clearly, and of course, all the streetlights across the street had burned out or were shot out. "Kids were talking and crying about his death at school today."

"Yeah, I know about it."

"They said he was slanging over on Virginia. Ain't that our street?"

"Yep, it is."

"So, do you think one of ours killed him or another gang?"

"Dude, we ain't no gang. We a family. That gang stuff played out."

"Well, what you think happened? Who you think hit him?"

"I'm sure we will never find out."

"How can you be so sure?"

"Because another Black drug dealer got knocked off. The cops don't care who did it. As long as another one of us is off the streets." Dymond took a long deep breath. "That's how this game works."

"I thought you said this wasn't no game."

"Oh, it's a game, alright, but just not something to be playing around with." He darted his eyes into mine. "That reminds me."

Dymond stood up and pointed to the side of the house, indicating for me to follow him. In the backyard, a dirty weather-beaten box sat nailed to a small tree. Loads of old leaves were stuffed in the box, and Dymond put his hand inside, and magically, a phone appeared. Then he pulled out another phone. Finally, he tugged a gun from the dilapidated birdhouse. He steered me toward the back porch.

This porch was wooden with chipped brown paint and splinters sticking out. We didn't sit down because the porch had no steps. Dymond passed me the items he retrieved from the birdhouse.

"This is a burner phone," he said. "You need to break it every night you use it, then throw the broken phone in a sewer or a Dumpster in an alley. You'll receive a new one every time you get rid of one. You only call me using this phone. Once you pick up regular customers, you can contact them with the burner phone."

He then handed me an iPhone. "Don't activate this until you are at home. Never bring this to the spot. Don't take it to school. These phones can be tracked, traced, and hacked. Nothing illegal should be done or said with this phone. This is for your personal calls and texts only."

"Wow! My first cell phone." I admired the phone like a Christmas present in November. "So how do I pay for this and the monthly payments?"

"Your next one hundred dollars goes to Monae. The phone is in her name. Every month you give her money for your bill. It's thirty-five each month. Don't worry about the burner phones. They will always be taken care of."

I started nodding my head in agreement. Dymond then grabbed the small silver barrel of the pistol and handed the black rubber handle to me. "This is your heater. A snub-nosed thirty-eight. You ever shoot a gun before?" It was kinda dirty.

I tried to sound confident, but my voice cracked a little. "No, not really." Actually, not at all. That was the first time I'd ever touched a real gun.

"Hell. I guess we gonna have to go practicing down at the river soon. You gotta know what you doing with this thing. Be careful cause it's all loaded and ready to go."

Again, I shook my head in approval. Holding this shiny piece of steel made me feel like I could conquer the world. Like I could do anything I wanted to do.

"Man, I appreciate this, Dymond."

"Bro, this is necessary. Like I said, fools trying to perch on top and stay on top. You gotta be prepared for anything." Dymond pointed his head toward the side of the house and began walking towards the front. "You ready?"

I nodded my head, mesmerized by the gun.

"I said, are you ready, Jay?"

I slipped out of my daydream and nodded my head again. "Oh, yeah, I'm ready for whatever," I said, as confidently as I could.

We went back to the front porch and sat waiting on our customers.

After a couple of hours, I wanted to leave. My fingers were brittle, and hardly any customers had made an appearance this dull Monday night. Then a car pulled up. Dymond said it was his customer, but I had never seen this particular car before. I couldn't stop admiring the pearl white Honda Civic Type R. This car could outrun almost any expensive sports car.

The car came to a purring stop with the continual beat of deep bass polluting the air. Dymond walked over to make the sale.

I couldn't keep my eyes off that slick car, but I got a little concerned because the sale was taking longer than usual. Then without warning, the vehicle took off, tires squealing on the rough pavement. The spoiler, the fins, and the dual exhaust pipes whizzed down the street, and the bass became muffled. Dymond suddenly displayed a baffled face as his gaze followed the white car down the dark road.

Seconds later, the quick tweets of sirens resonated. A cop car and an unmarked police car from either direction hummed towards Dymond and came screeching to a halt. Dymond took off like a jet as he ran in between two houses and into the backway alley. The cops jumped out of their cars and gave chase.

The dim porch light flicked off, and the door squeaked open. "Drop the stuff in the mail slot."

I turned around and observed who I figured was Monae, peering through the slit of the door. "Hurry up, boy: the gun, the phones, and the weed. You got any money on you, put that in there too. And don't stand up."

The door quietly closed. I stayed on my butt and scooted towards it. I snatched everything out of my pants' pockets and the pocket in my hoodie and stashed everything through the mail slot on the door. I expected a crash as the items hit the floor, but I heard nothing. The stuff must have dropped on the carpet or something. Suddenly, through the partially opened door, a muffled voice emerged again. "Sit on the steps, and don't say nothing."

A few minutes later, two White cops and a Black one ran back to their cars. One of the White cops looked toward me. He did a double-take and said something to the two other police officers.

They got in a car together and drove off while the lone cop strode towards me. My stomach was doing backflips. My forehead got hot. Moisture flooded my cheek. Fear gripped my entire body as the White police officer pointed his flashlight and his gun directly at my face.

CHAPTER 11 ~ Kamree

✳✳✳✳✳✳✳✳✳

For some reason, I couldn't stop thinking about Jayrin. I'd known him since we were young, and I always felt he was a cool kid from school. Like a play brother. We were close, but not that close. Just close enough that we could hold a decent conversation with one another and hang around each other at school. Eventually, I convinced him to go to church with me and my family a few times.

Our friendship grew, but in the eighth grade, he started hitting on me. I guess I took his desperate attempts as merely silly jokes. Lately, I had been wondering if his comments were real and how I felt about them. He'd been heavily on my mind all day. I couldn't sleep because he flooded my thoughts. I didn't understand why. Since this sleepless turmoil involved a boy, I figured I'd go to the expert for advice.

Me: *Prina, are you up?*

My phone's screen showed the time was shortly after eleven o'clock, but I knew she didn't go to sleep too early. What was taking her forever to respond to my text?

Me: *Hey Prina.*

Kaprina: *yeah, wats up?*

Me: *I need to talk to you about something.*

Kaprina: *what is it?*

Me: *Were you sleep?*

Kaprina: *nope. 'bout to tho*

Me: *Ok, I'll be quick. I've been crushing on this boy lately, and I don't know what to do about it.*

Kaprina: *a boy? who?*

Me: *You would never guess.*

Kaprina: *that's cause i ain't tryna guess*

Me: *It's Jayrin.*

Kaprina: *jayrin? omg. r u serious?*

Me: *Yeah, girl. I don't know why I'm feeling like that, but I am.*

Kaprina: *but you been knowin' him forever. how you finally now crushin on him like that?*

Me: *I know, right?*

Kaprina: *so what u gon do? u tellin' him?*

Me: *I don't know. I mean, he always be acting like he's trying to get with me. Maybe I should wait till he says something to me again and then actually take him up on his offer.*

Kaprina: *look at u. only broke up with Tra a couple of weeks ago and u already jumpin' on sumthin' else. u stepping up yo game, Kam. u shouldn't w8 on him tho, u need to say sumthin' to him right away b4 somebody else try to snatch him up*

Me: *Like who? Nobody's trying to get with Jayrin.*

Kaprina: *idk. ijs, stuff like that happens all the time and as soon as you think about doing sumthin', it can b 2 late.*

Me: *Yeah, I guess you're right. I'll probably say something to him tomorrow at school.*

Kaprina: *ok tell me how it goes*

Me: *Ok!*

Sleep evaded me, but since I wasn't going to school the next day, anyhow, I laid there in my bed. I couldn't possibly fall asleep anyway, considering how loudly my parents were arguing. I couldn't quite determine the subject of this particular argument, but it seemed very intense. My father's baritone bass voice swallowed up the shrill inflection of my mom's.

The bickering took me back again to that time they were finally going to tell me the circumstances they had been keeping from me for so long.

✱✱✱✱✱✱✱✱✱

"Fine," my father said. "I'll tell him."
Mom shook her head in disagreement. "James, I don't like it when this comes up in conversations. I don't want to think about it. I don't want to hear it. So, I'm going to the bedroom."

"No, Trista, you need to be here for this. To make sure I get this right. We can support each other while the truth comes out."

"But this truth is a dark moment for me, James. You know how it brings up deep pain." A tear puddled in my mom's eye but remained there, like a shallow pool. "This is not just about Aceson knowing the truth. This truth also does something to me!" she continued.

A dark moment? Deep pain? I thought I could handle it, but then I began thinking this might not be such a good idea after all.

"After this, we won't bring it up again. We need to tell the boy, or he will live with a sense of doubt forever. The best thing is the truth comes out and suffocates all the darkness lingering in the atmosphere. That's what the truth does; it sheds light."

"Well, hell, who made you Aristotle? I guess you got the answers to global warming as well, too?"

My dad chuckled. "I'm glad you can make light of a serious situation." He peeked at me and then continued. "Look, we are a family, and we need to get through this as a family. If you insist on leaving, go right ahead. Keep in mind we need to be here for each other at times like this. I promise this will not make things worse."

My mom stood from the dinner table, and my dad's eyes trailed her actions. My eyes followed his. Mom grabbed the dinner glasses and put them in the sink. She began clearing the other dishes while my dad and I sat silent and still. Eventually, she sat back down at the table with us and motioned her hand to my dad, as if to say, *go right ahead, the floor is yours.*

Dad took in a tiny breath. "Ace, what we will tell you devastated us, as your mother alluded. However, we want you to understand why we had no other children after you." I shot a glance at my mom to see her facial expression. She looked stoic. Her eyes dead. "You see, your mother and I tried to have kids before we had you. She became pregnant twice." Another glimpse at my mom.

"Unfortunately, both times, the babies died. One was a miscarriage. You know what having a miscarriage means?"

I nodded.

"The second baby died soon after it was born."

"After *she* was born," my mother cut in.

"After she was born." Dad cleared his throat. "As you can imagine, that wrecked us. Nevertheless, we tried once more, and as a result, we were blessed with you."

Wow, for once in my life, I considered myself wanted. I've always thought I disappointed everyone, but I figured after losing out on two other kids, even I would be a welcomed sight.

"My attitude toward having children changed after that," my mother interrupted, "and I didn't want to try again. I didn't want to risk being heartbroken from losing another child. I would not have been able to go through that hell again—"

"*We* would not have been able to go through that again," my father cut in.

Mom pursed her lips and gave Dad a side-eye.

"We understand how kids sometimes want companionship. A natural longing that kids have, wanting a sibling. Some want a puppy or a kitten, but you wanted a baby brother or sister. We believed we could not give that to you, so we didn't try. I did think about adoption at one time, but your mother didn't think so highly about that idea, either."

"No, I didn't. I figured every time I would look at a child we adopted, it would remind me that I failed."

My eyes jolted towards my mom when I heard her admission of failure. I thought I was the failure in the family. My mom always appeared to be flawless. A perfect wife. Surprisingly, she didn't feel that way about herself.

****

Somehow, my parents survived their trauma and stayed together. It seemed they were barely hanging on by a thread, though. I had to admit I did many stupid things; my parents expressed their disappointment with me. Often. I sometimes wondered if their fights were the culmination of two babies' deaths they wished they had. Or about the one son they sometimes wished they didn't.

The cop's flashlight blinded me. I squinted hard enough to give myself a slight headache, but through the squint, there was no mistaking that his deathly gun, in his other hand, remained fixed on my forehead. His lips parted, ready to speak when the squeaky door interrupted him.

"Boy, get in here! It's almost eleven o'clock. You know you gotta wake up early and go to school in the morning."

I didn't turn around because I refused to take my partially eclipsed eyes off the piece of steel that stared at me.

"Oh, officer," Monae continued, "I didn't see you. Is there a problem?"

The cop seemed hesitant to answer as he eyed me, then wickedly examined Monae with a scrunched up, unsure face. "Is this your home, ma'am?"

"Yes, it is," Monae responded.

"Is this your son?" he asked, still with a puzzled expression.

"Oh, no, officer," Monae said with a superficial chuckle. "He's my little brother. I'm taking care of him since our mom is sick and is no longer able to."

I tried not to appear surprised, even though her words completely caught me off guard.

"Who's the other boy who sat here with you?" The cop was looking at me again.

"Don't speak, Jayrin. You are a minor, and you are not obligated to talk to him," Monae said, as her dark brown eyes pierced through the officer's eyes.

"You don't want to obstruct an investigation," the officer

growled.

"What investigation?"

At that point, my head was swiveling back and forth, listening to the two of them volley words like two angry, grunting tennis players.

"That other boy was selling drugs and then took off running, basically resisting arrest. We need to identify who he is and where he lives."

With that, the only sounds igniting the night-time air were the chirping crickets and the booming traffic on Grand Avenue. Monae stared at the cop, waiting for him to say something else.

"So, you're not telling me who he is?" the officer asked.

"I don't know who he is or where he stays."

"Really? You just let strangers sit on your porch?"

Monae pursed her lips, tilted her head, and retorted, "You're a stranger, and you on my porch, ain't you?"

The officer turned his heinous face toward me. I sheepishly looked away. The rotating blades of a helicopter came and lingered in the air. My eyes squinted up at the bright eye of the dirty bird, which beamed down, apparently searching for someone, probably Dymond.

The officer followed my gaze and peeped at the light as well. "Fine. Whatever. We'll catch up to you scum sooner or later." He turned quickly, spat in the dead lawn, and hopped in his dark-colored Ford Crown Victoria.

Dangit! How did I miss that car?

"Jayrin, you need to come in here," I heard Monae say behind me.

I walked through the door, and what I viewed startled

me. Light gray painted walls outfitted with beautiful paintings, expensive-looking leather furniture, and a television about the size of the wall; the room was the exact opposite of the house's outside. The exterior resembled a dump. The inside imitated a small palatial dwelling. The TV displayed a quad split-screen view to all four sides outside of the house. Monae shook me out of my awe when she practically shoved me in a plush chair.

"You messed up, Jayrin."

The statement baffled me.

"You have to keep your head on a swivel. There's no way that you shouldn't have seen those cop cars."

"How did you see..." my voice trailed off as I glanced at the dynamic full-screen television. "Oh." I felt dejected.

"Y'all gotta look out for each other. If not, somebody gonna get caught up."

I put my head in my hands. "I hope Dymond's alright," I said with fear in my voice.

"He gon' be fine, this time. He can outrun all those stupid, fat cops. But next time, he may not be so lucky," she warned.

CHAPTER 14 ~ Kamree

It was lunchtime, and I was looking for Jayrin but didn't see him in the cafeteria. Usually, I would see him at the beginning of lunch, but by the time lunch was over, I wouldn't have a clue as to where he was. With the loud talking, obnoxious laughing, and indistinct noises, I tried to concentrate and focus on finding Jayrin.

"Prina, have you seen Jayrin?"

"Nope. But then again, I wasn't looking for him either."

"You're no help." Prina was too wrapped up with the other four or five girls sitting at the table. Nobody was really eating anything. Most of the time, we just bought some Red Hot Riplets potato chips and a Vess soda. And then we were on our phones, checking social media for the majority of lunchtime. I kept scanning the room, looking for Jayrin's black hoodie and black jeans or sweatpants to make an appearance. Poor boy. That's pretty much all he wore every day.

"Is that him walking out?" Prina asked. I say one thing about Kaprina: she can be totally enveloped in one thing and have the sense to move to another thing at the drop of a dime.

"Yep, that's him!" I rose from the table, almost stumbling on the leg of the chair. He was going upstairs to the main hall glancing behind him. He spotted me and stopped on the top step as I waved him down.

"Hey, hey, what's up Kam?"

"Nothing, what's up with you?

"Nothing for real."

"Where are you going?"

"Um, I'm just... I gotta go take care of some business."

"What kind of business?"

A moment of silence sliced through us even though the decibel meter was on one hundred behind us in the cafeteria.

"Did you want something?" he asked, looking up the stairs.

"I did want to talk to you about something, but dang, you act like you really gotta go."

"I mean, I do. But check it out. I got my own phone now. Let me give you my number. Hit me up tonight."

I glanced at him quizzically as he ran off his digits. I put his number in my phone and saved it in the contacts.

"Okay, I got it," I said, sounding disappointed. "I'll call you now, so you'll know my number when I call."

"Aight, cool. Like I said, hit me up like around eleven."

"Okay, I will."

He shot up the stairs, and I stood there at the bottom, not knowing where he was going. But something told me it wasn't anywhere good.

"So, what you say to Jayrin?" Prina asked me when I got back to the table.

"Nothing. Just that I wanted to talk to him."

"And what he say?"

"He had to go, so he told me to call him later tonight. On his cell phone."

Prina looked at me like I was crazy. "He got a phone?"

"Yep."

"How in the hell he get a cell phone?"

"I don't know, but he's always talking about his mom working two jobs, so maybe she made enough money to get him one." I didn't know if I believed myself when I said that.

✱✱✱✱✱✱✱✱

On Tuesday, I played video games like I had no place to go, which happened to be true. Living in teenage heaven, playing video games and eating potato chips in my bed all day. What took me so long to get suspended? This was the best.

Then the best turned into the worst. The sound of the alarm startled me again. What part of 'I don't need a babysitter' didn't he get? Gosh.

"Got something for you," my dad called out.

Maybe this wasn't so bad after all.

"Oh yeah! What?" I yelled as he appeared in my room.

Eyes still glued to the television, fingers still stuck to the controller, I heard a thud next to me on the bed. To my disappointment, books and papers flooded the area right on top of my chips. Smashed them into tiny pieces.

"Stopped by your school to retrieve the schoolwork you're missing this week. So, shut down the game, and let's get to work. Looks like a lot."

My entire world was just smashed into tiny pieces.

"Now?" I whined.

"Why not?" he asked.

"Today's Tuesday. Can't I work on all this the rest of the week and the weekend?"

"No, because you would easily procrastinate and wait until Sunday evening to start. Begin now, do some every day, and before Sunday gets here, you should be all done."

I sighed. "All right," I said as I turned the game off.

"Ace, I trust you're going to do the right thing. It's almost 11:30. You can eat something," he said, as he turned up a nose to the crumbled chips on my bed, "and then do some work until 3:30. You can play video games when I come home from work. For one hour."

"That's all? One hour?"

"Yes, for one hour. You will not drown yourself in this game this week. You're lucky I'm allowing you to play that dumb game at all. Sixty minutes a day. Do you understand?"

"Yes, I understand," I said.

"When I get home."

"Okay." I sounded like a whiney baby.

"And you know what else?"

I unceremoniously shook my head.

"You need to wake up at the same time you would on a regular school day, have breakfast, put on clothes, wash up, and start doing your homework immediately. For the rest of the week, you're going to go through this routine."

I got suspended for nothing. This was crazy.

"Okay, Dad, if you say so," I mumbled dryly.

He glanced at me again, lips twitched to say something else but instead walked out of the room.

I could not remember the last time we had engaged in a decent conversation—just him and me. My dad worked so much or went out of town on business trips, and whenever he came home from work, he ate dinner and went to sleep.

If I were an athlete, he would probably have never come to a game, or if I played an instrument, he'd never come to a concert—no time to sit and talk or go outside and play catch or anything. I couldn't understand how a father didn't want anything to do with his son.

Even when he was there, he was invisible.

CHAPTER 16 ~ Jayrin

✳✳✳✳✳✳✳✳

We had to go to a different spot. The front of Monae's house was a hot spot and off-limits for a while. This new location was a few blocks from her house. I asked Dymond how we would handle the money drop and everything, and he said it was the same way, just at a different crib.

"Whose house is this?"

"Don't worry about it. This is a temporary arrangement. We'll be here for a couple of days, and then we're out. No need to be caught up in whose house this is." Dymond said this with a mean mug. He didn't pay much attention to me. His gaze was mainly on the activity of a few people walking on the block—no idle chatter whatsoever between us.

Somebody walked up to the house, and Dymond was familiar with this person because he and Dymond strolled the sidewalk for a short moment and engaged in an exchange.
Not many customers came to me. It seemed like all the cars that rolled up belonged to Dymond. I asked him why so many of his customers came to the new spot.

"I called them and told them where to meet me," he said with a clenched jaw.

"Dang it, I didn't do that. You think, maybe I could sell to one of your regulars?"
Dymond glared at me like I was a four-year-old kid asking to drive a car. "No. Most of mine ain't buying weed."

"What you mean?"

"I'm serving mostly meth, heroin, prescription pills."
I thought back to the helicopter shining its light. Maybe they were looking for Dymond because he wasn't just selling weed.

He was slanging some heavy stuff. Dymond didn't look at me. "For real?" I squealed. "Well, can I—"

"No!" Dymond cut me off. Then he set his piercing eyes on me. "You just a little street soldier. Street soldiers only handle weed. If the cops arrest you with a couple bags of weed, charges ain't nothing. Arrested with what I'm carrying..." He shook his head slowly. "Nah. You can't push nothing to none of my customers." He turned back to the block.

I had no idea Dymond sold other drugs. No wonder he was raking in so much more money. I needed to try to sell that stuff too. I needed more funds to help my mom provide for us. I wanted to cop me some new clothes and new shoes.

Thankfully, a few random customers finally came, and I was able to make a little money. Then out of nowhere, I remembered Kamree said she'd call me at eleven. At about 10:50, I told Dymond I had to leave. He told me to go. I left; he had been acting like he didn't want me at the new post anyway.

As soon as I walked in the house, my mom stepped into the hallway. "Jay, you need to come to my room." She still had on her work clothes. Usually, she would be getting ready for bed at that time. She wanted me in her room, undoubtedly, to talk to her about something important.

"Okay." I stopped by my room to dump off a few things and to grab something else.

"Yes, Momma."

"Son, I need to talk to you about something." I was not in the mood for serious talking. "Sit down on my bed." Mom petted the mattress like it was a soft dog. I sat down with my hands inside the pockets of my hoodie.

"It's almost eleven o'clock on a school night. I don't understand why you are coming home every night so late."

"Well, I don't got no curfew," I said calmly. "You've never told me I had to be in at a certain time."

"And if I did, would you come in at that time?"
I shrugged my shoulders.

"What are you doing, causing you to stay out so late?"

"Hanging out with my friends."

"Friends? What friends?"

"Dang! Mom, you act like I ain't got no friends."

"Who are they?"

I was thinking about my cell phone and how Kamree was going to be calling soon. I had to end this conversation swiftly.

"Dymond—"

"I figured you've been with that no-good, low-life thug."

"Whoa, why you all on Dymond like that? Do you even know him like that?"

"I knew about his father. I remember his brother. So yeah, I do understand what he's about. What y'all out there doing? Loitering in the streets, selling drugs, I bet."

"Why you think that?"

"What else are you doing? You still haven't answered?"
I didn't like lying to my mom. I gingerly pulled my hands out of my pocket, gripping neatly folded bills, and then extended my hand towards her like a peace offering. I didn't say anything, and she didn't offer her hand to my implied invitation.

"Are you kidding me?" she asked me with pursed lips.
I couldn't look her in the eyes, and I left my arm stretched out with the cash.

"So, where are you getting this money from? You *are* selling drugs."

I tilted my head as to say *I don't want to say it, but you know.* I swallowed hard.

"No need to say anything; I smell it on you." Guilt ravaged my face, and I still couldn't force myself to consider her eyes for more than a nanosecond. "Jayrin, I'm not taking your money," she said.

"Why?" I quickly realized I said that with attitude.

"Because it's drug money, Son!"

"It's just weed, Mom," I whined.

"Boy, I'm not subjecting myself, my kids, my household to the curse of that evil money."

"Even though your household and your kids need it. Tell me we couldn't use this cash."

"We could use some money, but not *this* money. We don't need it. I work two jobs to make sure you, your brother, and your sister have everything you need." I gave her a side-eye, but she continued. "You eat food every day, with a place to sleep and a closet full of clothes."

"Mom, my clothes are trash. You got them from the thrift shop, and my brother has to wear them when they get too small for me. That ain't no way to be living."

"Boy, you just don't know how many people do live like that."

"Well, I don't want to be one of them."

"That's why you are at a great school, so you can receive a better education, go to college, obtain a degree or two, and then land a fine job so you can earn enough money to buy whatever clothes you want, the right way."

My mom once told me how she got pregnant with me when she was in her third year of college but had to drop out after I was born. She fell eighteen hours short of a nursing degree. She wanted to be a nurse practitioner. Without completing school, she eventually got a job as a medical assistant. It didn't pay enough to support three kids, so she started working weekends at a corner market after the twins were born.

"That's later in the distant future. But what about now?"

"You want to help. Why don't you go get a real job? You're fifteen. You can be hired somewhere."

"At my age, the only thing I can do is work fast food. I ain't doing that."

"Yeah, I thought so. Your talk is cheap, and your walk is weak."

Dang! Did my mom just throw shade at me?

"If you were serious about doing something, you would be willing to work wherever and do what you had to do."

"I am doing what I have to do."

"And by doing that, you're going to get yourself killed. Or locked up. Even though recreational marijuana is legal in some states, like across the river in Illinois, weed on the street is still illegal in Missouri. So dead or in jail, the option is up to you. You used to be such a good boy. But bad company corrupts good character. And that's what's happening to you. You need to choose to do the right thing, Jayrin. We all make life-changing decisions, decisions which could change our lives either for better or for worse."

This made me think back to the decision my mom made the day I was born. I reminisced again about that talk I had with her a few years ago.

✳✳✳✳✳✳✳✳

"What do you mean he didn't know if you were going to keep me?"

"Well, while I was pregnant, I had planned to give you up for adoption. All plans ready to go. The adopting couple drove down from Chicago, waiting for you to be born. However, after I asked the nurse to let me see you, all the pain and anguish I felt were replaced with joy when you were born. And when I saw you for the first time and held you in my arms, there was no way I could give you up." My mom's eyes welled up. "This decision changed my life forever," she said.

"Yeah, it kept you from finishing school, and now you are paying for that decision."

"No, I'm not paying for anything. I am benefiting from my decision to have you and keep you. I could not imagine my life without you. I couldn't fathom life without Jaiyce or Jaiyde, either. Yes, I made the mistake of having my children without being married and with no support from your fathers, but you were not mistakes."

"Well, my so-called father must believe I was a mistake since he didn't want nothing to do with me."

"Your father—"

"Please, don't call him my father," I cut in.

"Well, he was under the impression you were going to be adopted—"

"That you were going to give me up to someone else," I sharply interrupted.

My mom turned uncomfortably on her bed, but she couldn't deny my emotions. She breathed in heavily and went on. "He expressed shock and anger when I contacted and informed him that I did not give you up."

"So, after you told him, why didn't he just face reality and decide to be my father?"

"It's complicated, Jayrin."

"You always say it's complicated, or I'm too young. But you always say how smart I am. I'm sure if you talk to me and tell me the truth, I would be able to understand."

Mom looked at me with a seriousness I had never seen before. She got up from the bed and studied herself in the mirror. Her room was small and neat but full of mismatched furniture: black bedpost, light brown dresser, dark almond nightstand, an imbalance of yard sales; Goodwill and other peoples' trashed furniture filled the room. Mom's creative mind made it work as if they all came from some fancy and expensive furniture store in West County.

She peeked in the mirror at my reflection and turned shyly. "The man was married when you were conceived."

My head started spinning. I took a hard swallow. A large stone pushed down my throat. My mom had already talked to me about sex, and the talk didn't help because she couldn't possibly understand my feelings about sex as a boy. But the fact that my father—the man she had sex with—had a wife shocked me so much that the voltage nearly stopped my heart.

****

"You are here because God saw fit that you should be here, so I am responsible for making sure you and your siblings are fulfilling all of what God wants for you. He did not give you life so you can be out there pushing drugs and frolicking with thugs."

"Nah, Mom. Don't come to me again with that God crap. Where is God when I need him? Where is God when you need him? I don't see God, just like I don't see my father. God is invisible to me. He ain't doing nothing for me," I said while getting up from her bed, ready to walk out. Her door was closed so the twins wouldn't come in unexpectedly. I swung the door open, and before I could muscle it past the halfway mark, her hand slapped it and slammed it shut.

It startled me.

"No, you are not going to talk crazy about God. You can be mad at me. You can be pissed at your father. But you better be grateful for what God has done for you."

"What, Mom! What has he done for me? We live in this old house in this piss-poor neighborhood. You work like a dog, and we still ain't got nothing. What I got to be grateful for?" I asked.

"Be thankful you have breath in your body and have air to breathe in, which, by the way, you can't see either. No, you don't wear the best clothes, but you have clothes. We've gone over this before. There are kids out there who wished they had what you have. Some of them living on the street. Literally. You don't realize how good you got it. I'm not going to pretend everything is roses, but I know everything ain't thorns either."

I stood, hand on the doorknob, prepared to depart from that room as soon as possible. Unfortunately, my mom's hand remained on the door, keeping me from escaping the deathly despair of her bedroom. I was enraged. I was done with God. Done with my father. Done with my mother. I was done.

"You can leave now," my mom said, "but don't bring that dirty money into this house. You wanna go out there and keep doing what you are doing, stay out there and do it, but don't come home putting me and your brother and sister in danger." She paused. "You need to make a hard decision. But this is your choice to make."

She quietly opened the door, and I loudly walked out. I got to my room and grabbed my phone. The screen lit up with *1 Missed Call.*

I also had a text message:

Kamree: *Jayrin, I tried to call you, but you didn't answer. I guess you are too busy at 11 o'clock at night so I won't bother you... anymore.*

I called her back, but after a few rings, it went to voicemail. I texted her:

Me: *Kam, i was talking to my mom...sorry i missed your call. I called you back. I'm still up, call me back*

It was 11:13. I waited for the call. 11:20. Nothing. 11:30. Nothing. Midnight... I guess I got ghosted.

CHAPTER 17 ~ Kamree

✹✹✹✹✹✹✹✹✹

What important business did Jayrin need to attend to at eleven o'clock on a school night? I began to wonder about him. He seemed to disappear from school often. And now he asked me to call him, and when I did, he didn't answer. Maybe all that talk meant nothing. Perhaps he didn't like me the way I thought he did. I probably made a fool of myself, thinking he could have been the one.

Kaprina's way of living proved to be right, after all. The one, Mr. Right, was not very likely to be found. Especially for kids like us. Why did I even need a stupid boyfriend? Just because everyone else wanted one? What a tremendously stupid reason. I considered myself better than that. I had more to live for than chasing around irrelevant, simple-minded little boys. I needed to get my stuff together.

Then my cell phone rang. Jayrin. My heart skipped a beat. I turned on the lamp, the light striking the darkness with hope. I sat up, wondering if I should answer the phone. I decided not to. Let him sweat a bit. The ringing stopped. A text soon followed:

Jayrin: *Kam, i was talking to my mom... sorry i missed your call. I called you back. I'm still up, call me back*

Talking to your mother? Why did I have a feeling he was lying to me? I dropped my phone on my bed, switched off my light, and cried myself to sleep.

CHAPTER 18 ~ Aceson

✳✳✳✳✳✳✳✳✳

Jealousy entrenched in me because most boys at my school bragged about how they played against each other on the Xbox. I sat in my X Rocker Black Leather Vibrating Gaming Chair, wishing I could be playing against someone. Well, I guess everyone else was at school, but it sucked that nobody had ever asked to play with me, and whenever I asked someone, they just laughed at me and kept walking.

There came a time when I would drown in boredom playing against the computer. But I had no choice. No brother to compete against. No friends. Heck, I even heard some guys say their dads sometimes played Xbox with them. My dad would never do a cool thing like that.

After waking up on this last day of my suspension, I did the whole, get-ready-to-go-to-school-but-not-go-to-school thing. Fortunately, I had finished all my homework for the week. I went downstairs and grabbed my lunch: chips, a soda, and of course, apple pie. Needed that serving of fruit.

Full of a hearty and healthy meal, I went upstairs to my room with nothing to do. The clock stared at me with its blue-flamed digital numbers. Not quite twelve-thirty. What was I to do for the next five or six hours until my father came home?

I reluctantly eyed the dusty bookshelf, and the books glared back at me with smirks. My useless pride took on the challenge and picked up one of the numerous books my mom had given me. She said reading all the kids' classics would put me ahead of other kids my age. *Treasure Island* found its way into my hands. I surveyed the novel. Opened it. Read the first sentence. Then guiltlessly shoved the book back on its wooden home. Dust balls smacked me in the face, and I spit furiously, regretting picking up the book in the first place.

I regarded my cell phone for no practical reason. My mom and dad added an app where I couldn't use screen time during school hours. Although I wasn't in school, it was still school hours.

Still searching for something to do, I glanced at the television, followed by my Xbox. The Xbox looked back at me. It spoke to me. And I did not ignore it.

Three hours later, my numb thumb urged me to rise and go to the bathroom. My bladder hit me like a punching bag, and I had waited so long, the intense sensation of peeing my pants was threatening. Stumbling off my mattress, I sensed the controller cord caught between my legs. I moved in slow motion, but everything around me developed in an ultra-fast-forward velocity.

The scene played out, and I wished the rewind button had magically appeared under my finger. It didn't. I thought back, thinking that I should have had wireless controllers. My parents said I could use my allowance to buy one, or I could wait, and they would give me one for Christmas. Well, I thought I would wait another month or so. That way, I didn't spend my own money. I was no dummy.

However, as I witnessed the Xbox slowly take a fast nosedive from my dresser, my stomach dropped at an equally quick pace, while my hands couldn't navigate through the invisible quicksand, which kept them from saving the day. The game's descent concluded with a clang on the hardwood floor.

It smashed into many microscopic pieces of plastic, and I let go of my wired controller in horror as the remains of my

Xbox crawled under my bed. My eyes trailed the wire from the Xbox to the controller. I rechecked the clock, then put my hand on my head in utter disgust.

Jeez, I was a dummy!

Part 2

Bright Darkness

"But for some reason, I couldn't pull the trigger."

~ Jayrin Foster

"I stay away from any and everything illegal."

~ Kamree Covington

"I laid down, closed my eyes as tight as I could, and wished to God I could disappear because I was tired of my life."

~ Aceson Denner

✱✱✱✱✱✱✱✱✱

I was just about to go back out to the spot when my mom came in from working her second job at the corner store. She got off at five o'clock from the clinic and then rode a bus to her weekend job at Penny's Corner Store, a block from our house. The store closed at nine o'clock, and it took Mom less than ten minutes to walk home. I tried to time my exit as she was coming home so I could sneak to the stoop and prepare for the late-night sales. Friday was always poppin' because the weed heads needed to get lit before hittin' the clubs.

"Should I ask where you are going, Jay?"

"Hanging out, Mom."

"Yeah, I know what that means." A long uncomfortable silence sliced through the frigid air on our front porch. "Well, you won't be going anywhere tonight, Mister. Come inside. We need to talk."

Again?

I huffed and reluctantly went back into the house and walked through our narrow, dark hallway. The light bulb had been out for a few weeks. Mom had asked me to change it many times, but I kept neglecting it. The darkness gave the aura of walking toward the unknown. I wondered what she wanted to talk about this time.

Mom grabbed my arm and told me to go to her room. She shut the door behind her. It was then I understood this would be another one of those talks. She didn't want Jaiyce and Jaiyde to hear what she had to say. I sat on her bed and the springs in the old mattress squealed.

"I got a call from your school today," she started. "I didn't take the call because I was working and couldn't leave the patient at the time. But the secretary left a message. She mentioned that you've been absent from many of your classes over the past several weeks. Apparently, someone's been skipping out on school."

Upon hearing this, my heart hardened.

She continued, "And this means I can find myself in legal trouble because of your truancy."

Then, my heart softened and became regretful.

"Now, I need to set an appointment to meet with your principal, counselor, and social worker sometime next week to come up with a plan to help you stay in school. That means taking off from work, missing out on money. If this continues, I could be sent to truancy court and be fined. Tell me, how in the world can I do this?"

Mom usually didn't yell at me, but she used a stern voice when she was serious. Sounded like a female drill sergeant without the animated facial features and flying spit.

"Why they put that all on you? What I did is not your fault," I said sympathetically, trying to take the heat off her and me.

"Because I'm your mother, and I'm still responsible for you. It doesn't matter how grown you think you are; you are still a child, my child."

I started rubbing my hands nervously and realized I had let my mom down. I choked out the next words. "I'm sorry, Mama. I'm sorry for everything."

"Well, if you're really sorry, you will stop hanging out in the street, quit hanging out with that fool, Dymond, stop selling drugs, and return to being serious with school."

For some reason, the mention of school stabbed me in my side. Throughout middle school, I was always a great student, mostly As and a couple of Bs. I enjoyed school, but when I began high school, I started hating it. I didn't want to be there. It wasn't only the drug scene that made me leave school every day. I simply didn't want to be there. Lost total interest. Didn't see the need.

"You used to love school. What's going on?"

"I'm sick of school. I don't really have any friends. Dymond is the only one who is there for me. The only one willing to help me out."

"What about Kamree? You two have been close since elementary school."

"Well yeah, Kamree's cool, but she always getting on my head about stuff. Don't want me to live my life." I started to say, *'just like you, Momma,'* but I didn't.

"But she's a good girl. Smart. Probably just wants you to be your best. Do your best at school. Just like I want you to."
I chuckled.

"Yeah, Kam is built for school. But I'm not. It comes easy for her. For me, it's becoming a struggle."

My mom rubbed her cheeks with both hands, up and down. She squinted her eyes hard. "It's a struggle because you're not interested in school. In learning. I recall taking you to the library every week and reading to you. You were extremely excited the first time you read to me. You would devour books about cars and trucks and trains. You started reading car magazines. What happened to that little boy?"

Since I could remember, I had been fascinated with automobiles. Makes and models of almost any car I saw were easily recognizable, and many times I could even guess the correct year of vehicles. I loved collecting pictures of car emblems. I would cut them out of magazines, newspapers; wherever I would see them, I'd try to get my hands on them.

"I'm still the same person, but I'm just not the same little boy," I responded.

At that moment, I felt a vibration in my pants pocket. My mom gave me a curious glance. She probably heard the slight buzz.

"Well, Son, you have some decisions to make, and you can start thinking about these decisions now because, like I said, you ain't going nowhere tonight. So get ready to join us for supper; it'll be ready in about fifteen minutes. I brought a box of macaroni from work, and we got some leftover chicken in the fridge. Yes, the hour is late, but we haven't had a good sit-down dinner as a family in a long time. I'll call you when the food is ready."

I stood and power-walked out of the room and didn't want her to hug me or nothing. I went to my room to answer Dymond's text. I knew he was trying to see where I was and what was taking me so long.

Ten minutes later, I had snuck out the house, and I was on Mildred Avenue telling Dymond how I wanted to go to the the mall.

"I can take you tomorrow. About noon."

"For real? Bet." It was time to cash in on some of my earnings and buy some new shoes and new clothes. After talking to my mom, I was really thinking about telling Dymond about quitting the game. But I was going to wait until after I got my fresh gear.

"Wait, bro, I didn't know you had a car."

✳✳✳✳✳✳✳✳✳

The vibration on my nightstand next to my bed startled me. It wasn't loud but loud enough to shake me from my deep sleep. I reached over and saw my screen. Jayrin. The time: twelve forty-seven. I should keep ignoring him and go back to sleep. But I had a feeling I would not be able to fall asleep thinking about Jayrin and wondering what we could have talked about. So, I answered the call.

"Why are you calling me so late?" I asked, trying to sound mad, but low-key, giddy he had called.

"I saw that you called me, so I'm calling you back. Made me feel good to see you thought about me, considering how you completely ignored me at school for the past few days."

"Ten o'clock is when I called you. It took you almost three hours to call me back. Let me guess, you were talking to your mom."

"Well, actually, I was—"

"Jayrin, I'm so tired of your lies."

"No, seriously, I was talking to my mom. I'm mean, not the entire time."

"So, what else have you been doing? And don't lie to me, Jayrin. I've been contemplating us getting together for real, but the way you've been acting, I'm beginning to second guess that thought, thinking we should continue being just friends. But now I'm beginning to rethink being friends."

A brief pause ensued. Jayrin huffed. "Okay," he started slowly. "I was hanging out on the block."

"Oh. On the block, huh? With whom? Doing what?"

"With Dymond."

I sat up in my bed. "Dymond!" I whispered violently. "Why are you hanging out with him?" I barked.

Jayrin didn't say anything. His silence spoke volumes.

"So that's why you always disappearing at school. Why you don't answer your phone late at night. Jayrin, everybody knows what Dymond does. Are you selling drugs?"

He remained silent. I should've hung up on him right then.

I grabbed my pillow and folded it into my belly. "Jayrin, I despise criminals. You know my daddy is locked up because he chose a life of crime over his family. I stay away from any and everything illegal. Jayrin, I ain't going out with no thug."

"I've been talking to my mom about it. She's been telling me I need to stop. So, yeah, I'm getting out. For real, for real. I'm telling Dymond tomorrow."

"I hope so, Jayrin. I would hate for ten years of friendship to go to waste."

CHAPTER 21 ~ Aceson

✷✷✷✷✷✷✷✷✷

Saturday mornings were usually unexcitable in our house, mainly because we would sit together and eat breakfast in an awkward hush. Me, my mom, and my dad, if he wasn't out doing business somewhere. No talking, only the clanging of silverware colliding with bowls and plates. But that Saturday morning displayed enough excitement to warrant fireworks. Anything but boring.

Walking downstairs, I heard my parents arguing again. Their bickering proved to be a beneficial event. Served as an excellent distraction when I told Dad about my broken Xbox. He would be too mad at Mom to assert his anger at me. Perfect timing. I hoped.

"Dad, I have something to tell you," I said, trembling.

"Yeah, what is it?"

"I... um... I broke my Xbox yesterday." I stuffed some golden scrambled eggs in my mouth quickly, hoping it would cover up what I just said.

"Really. Why am I not surprised? What happened?"

"I was trying to get up to go to the bathroom, and the controller cord got tangled around me, and... well, it fell."

"So, you were playing the game? What time did that happen?"

Dang. Lying by saying the incident occurred later in the afternoon was the first thing I had thought of. Although, I convinced myself that falsifying my day wouldn't do any good. My mouth sighed. If I was going to start trying to do right, I guess that was the perfect time to begin. "About 10:30." My head magnetized toward my mom, who appeared angry and sympathetic at the same time.

"I told you not to play the game until I came home."

"Yeah, but I finished all my work. I had nothing—"

My father began blinking rapidly and biting his lip. "Ace, I simply don't understand. You always find a way to disappoint me."

My mom cut in: "At least he took the initiative to tell you the truth."

"Am I supposed to give him some sort of award because he told the freaking truth for once?" my dad barked.

"Well, saying something positive to your son every once in a while, couldn't hurt," my mom snapped.

Yes! They were still angry at each other.

"Trista, don't tell me how to talk to him. He's been a knucklehead since he was born, and he hasn't thought to stop being one yet."

My mouth attacked the food faster, hoping to exit the hostile environment soon, so they could continue their squabble and leave me alone.

"Talking to him the way you are is not helping."

"Well, what will help? You got the answers? You know, I've been waiting for years for the perfect answer to his problems."

I wolfed down the remainder of my breakfast, binged my orange juice, and expeditiously put my dishes in the sink. Meanwhile, my parents kept going back and forth. My dad said something and yelled, and then my mom returned with words and grunted. I snuck past them and quietly ran upstairs to my room.

My plan had worked. At least I hoped it did.

"I'll be back."

"Where you going?" My sister Jaiyde was paper-thin, dark with a hundred pigtails and barrettes in her dark hair. An explosion of every color imaginable.

"I'm going to the mall."

"You know Mama don't like you leaving us home by ourselves," my brother Jaiyce chimed in.

"I will be back in no time. Way before Mama gets home. I'll even bring y'all something." Jaiyce and Jaiyde sat at the table, eating cereal. A weekly Saturday morning ritual, except usually I'd be eating with them. But my energy was on a hundred, knowing I would be buying new gear at the mall. Dymond said he would pick me up at ten. Mom worked from nine to three in the afternoon. She had already left for work.

"Trying to bribe me won't work." Although Jaiyce and Jaiyde were twins, they acted nothing alike. Jaiyce never smiled. Even though I knew he had two big buck teeth in the middle of his grill. He constantly wore a scowl on his face that resembled a boxer stepping into the ring, sizing up his opponent. His short haircut barely disclosed his woolly hair. And he didn't like me getting away with nothing.

"We'll be alright. Since you're bringing us something back, we will be okay—besides, we almost ten. Anybody who is double digits should be able to stay home by themselves," Jaiyde declared, in her usual animated, carefree way.

Jaiyce's squinting eyes partially revealed his piercing pupils peering deeply inside of mine. Jaiyce wasn't a great student in school, but I believed he possessed more street smarts than I did at his age. Something different hid behind his natural pout. I could tell he knew something. Like I had a sixth sense that he had a sixth sense. "You know mama ain't gonna be happy about this," Jaiyce said.

"Jaiyde is right, lil bro. Y'all will be alright. I'll be gone for about an hour or two. You have nothing to worry about. Go ahead and finish your breakfast and then go watch some TV or go play your game."

Jaiyce clenched his teeth and crossed his arms. I gingerly brushed his shoulder as I walked past him. I winked at Jaiyde and smiled, trying to match her bright beaming grin. Hers, real. Mine, fake.

A few minutes later, Dymond texted me saying he'd pulled up. His car was cool. A green Honda Accord. 2015. Not something I would expect a drug dealer to be riding in, though.

"Man, I wish I had a car. First, I gotta get my permit, but my mom would never let me. We ain't even got no car."

Dymond pulled off. I put my seat belt on and peeked at him. He didn't have his on, and I started to ask him about it but decided not to. Didn't want to sound lame.

"Bro, you don't need your mom."

"What you mean?"

"Monae can hook you up. She'll help you get one."

"For real?"

"On God, she can. You just gotta bring a phone bill or electric bill. Something official with your address on it. You also need your birth certificate."

Dymond didn't seem to be the best driver, and I had hoped he would not jump on the highway. But he did. Biting my nails, I looked at the steering wheel. I watched as his hands slid up and down the circular wheel. He wore gloves as usual. The temperature was cool, a little chilly, but I didn't think it was cold enough to wear gloves.

The speakers were rattling. I wanted to ask him to turn down the music because it was making me uneasy. The shrilling sounds of the music made me jittery. Besides, I wanted to tell Dymond about what I had discussed with my mom and Kamree; about no longer selling, but the loud sound aided my hesitance. It was the perfect excuse for staying silent. So telling him after he took me to buy clothes would be the best option.

While at the mall, I got a bunch of clothes for me, Kamree, Jaiyce, and Jaiyde. I bought my first pair of Jordans, and I wore them out of the store. I didn't get anything for my mom. She would bug out if I did. Dymond walked out of the mall with more bags than he could carry. That dude got so much money.

On the way back home, the music echoed at a much lower volume. It proved to be an excellent time to talk to Dymond. Every time I began to speak, I silently punked myself out of it. Why was I so scared to tell him I wanted out? Did I think this was a gang? Blood in, blood out? Did I think I would get jumped for leaving? But he said it wasn't a gang.

After thinking about it, I realized I could be a liability to Dymond, Monae, and whoever else they were working with. I knew where they kept the dope. I was familiar with how and where they dropped the money. Maybe if I told Dymond I wasn't going to slang dope no more, he would have to do something to me so that I wouldn't be able to snitch on the operation. That would not be best for me.

My reluctance to talk opened up the door for Dymond to

speak instead. "So, we are going to stay on the block till about eleven tonight, and then I got something else for you to do later on."

This confused me and frightened me. What in the world did he want me to do? "Oh yeah? What is it?" I replied.

"We gonna go checking car doors."

I felt like I was putting together a puzzle with a thousand pieces. I just wanted to put the pieces back in the box because I had no clue. "What you mean?"

"We going out to the county and check to see if any cars are unlocked." Some parts of St. Louis County were considered more upscale than St. Louis City. Many bouts of "White Flight" had White families leaving the city for supposedly better living out in the county. St. Louis was divided by a well-known street, Skinker Boulevard, that separated the county from the city.

"To steal them?" I asked carefully.

"Nah, man. To see what's in them. Take money or whatever else."

"You do this all the time?"

"Yep. I've gotten laptops, guns, cash; these stupid people be leaving wallets in their cars and don't lock the doors. So, yeah, I do it all the time."

"Why you asking me to go then?"

"Time to move on to new ways of getting money."

That statement marked a good time for me to say that I didn't want new ways of making money. I didn't want to make any more money, at least not illegally. I told Kamree I would leave the game, and this opportunity to inform Dymond sat in my hands. But for some reason, I couldn't pull the trigger.

Desperately, I wanted to call Jayrin but also didn't want to at the same time. My feelings for him jumped over an imaginary line. I had always thought of him as a genuinely good friend, my best male companion, but then I started feeling differently. Had I let all his teasing and fake flirting win me over?

I looked past his old clothes and worn-out shoes and recognized he was a cute boy. He was silly, serious, smart. Not a typical tough guy, which made me wonder why he started selling drugs and hanging out with Dymond. Though Dymond was supposedly bright like the rest of us, his reputation and the fact he came from a bad family swallowed his intelligence. Jayrin, on the other hand, always portrayed himself as a good kid.

In the end, I gave in to my urge to phone him. Even though I talked to him thousands of times throughout the years, my stomach tightened in anticipation of calling him. I kept picking up the phone, clicking on his name in my contacts, and putting the phone down. I would pick it up again and again without ever pulling the trigger. Finally, I pushed the button.

"Hello."

"Jayrin?"

"What's up, Kamree?"

"What are you doing?" My finger gripped my hair, twirling my curls in my right hand.

"Umm... on my way home from the Galleria. What you doing?"

"Galleria. How did you get to the Galleria?"

"Dymond."

My gut experienced a slight pull when I heard Dymond's name.

"I thought you were going to stop hanging out with him, Jayrin."

"Yes, I am, after tonight."

An exasperated sigh escaped my lips. "So why did you go to the mall with him?"

"He got a car, and he said he would take me."

"Dymond has a car? Ain't he fifteen?"

"Yep, but he'll be sixteen in a few months."

"But he's not old enough to have a driver's license; how he got a car?"

"Don't know. I didn't ask a bunch of questions like you doing now."

It was clear Jayrin's irritation mirrored my own. "I thought you were going to end this, Jayrin."

"I will. Tonight. There's nothing to worry about. I promise."

A slight rush of relief swarmed over me. He sounded sincere. I wanted to believe him.

"I bought you something—a button-down camo jacket. The girl at Forever 21 said you would be killing it with this on. If you want, I can bring it by tomorrow."

I didn't know how I felt about that. Sure, I could always use new clothes, but I didn't actually want to accept any gift from Jayrin. I also didn't want to hurt him. But for him to think about me was sweet.

"How considerate of you." I didn't realize I had stopped twirling my hair until I realized I had started twisting it again, this time with my left hand, my phone in my right hand. "However, I don't think I can take the jacket."

"What? Why? I mean, how can you turn down a gift? Dang, ain't you supposed to be my girl?"

My ear caught wind of mumbling. "What was that?"

"Dymond asking me if you were really my girl."

"Am I?" I asked, not sure myself.

"Ain't you?"

"Well, if we both need to ask, then the answer is probably no."

"So, that's why you won't take the jacket?"

"Well, because I don't think I want to take anything you got with that money."

"That money? You sound like my mama."

"Well, obviously, me and your mama are right."

"What does it matter? I already bought it. It's not stolen or nothing."

"No, but the principle of the thing makes it not right."

"Yeah, of course not. Miss Goody-Two-Shoes. Always gotta try to do the right thing."

"You say that like there's something wrong with that."

"No, but there is something wrong with somebody who thinks they are perfect. Trying to be better than everybody else. Someone who can't do nothing wrong."

Even though he used a double negative, I knew what he meant, and it kind of stung. For him to have thought that about me made me feel small. We never seemed to have these simple arguments when I was content with being Jayrin's friend. Once I decided to agree to date him, we started having these differing opinions, which led to little disagreements about everything.

The biggest issue, however, undoubtedly had to be him selling drugs. It didn't make me the bad person because I refused to be involved with someone who wanted to sell narcotics. It was illegal and dangerous. What if somebody wanted to come after him? Kill him?

Being Black in this city already had its destructive disadvantages. It implied fearing being shot for no reason, and selling drugs gave people a reason to shoot at you: cops, other drug dealers, drug fiends. Jayrin put himself and anybody with him in danger, including me!

So, it couldn't have been wrong for me to want him to stop? I think not. If he didn't understand that, and if he thought I was trying to be better than other people, he was stupid. I didn't try to be better than other people. I just tried to be better for myself; I tried to do better, hoping other people would try to do better too. I didn't want to repeat what my momma did; get with someone who wanted to be a thug more than wanting to be a father. And if Jayrin, of all people, didn't understand that, then he wasn't probably stupid. He was definitely stupid.

"I'll call you later, Jayrin, maybe."

"Wait, Kam—"

"Have fun with your homeboy."

I couldn't take it anymore. I hung up on him!

"Aceson, I'll be out of town all next week." I didn't break my gaze from my book. Since my Xbox was obliterated, I decided to punish myself and read *Treasure Island* after all. The novel didn't exactly hold my attention, where I couldn't tear away from it. I simply didn't want to regard my dad.

Numb to the late working hours, the business trips, I didn't understand why he told me these things. I didn't care. "I'm asking you, no, I'm begging you to be on your best behavior for your mother and at school." I held back a deep chuckle as I knew that my best behavior was still nothing to brag about. "You need to let this be the week you turn things around," he continued. "I don't want to talk to your mom on the phone and hear that you messed up again."

Messed up again? Geez. Life must be great to be someone who never messed up a day in their life.

Despite my hostility toward my dad, I did love him for some reason. Overall, he gave the impression of a decent man, just not that exceptional of a father. He owned his business for over ten years, always provided for Mom and me.

"Sure, Dad, I'll be on my best behavior."

"I mean it, Ace." I carried on with fake-reading the book. "Honestly, your mom hasn't been doing so well lately. I don't know what's wrong with her, but you having a good week could help her do better, and I'm sure if you add stress to her life, it won't be pleasant for her."

I closed my eyes so tight, hoping it would make him disappear. I squeezed them open quickly and realized he had not left. The disappointment flowed over me, but I tried to appease him so he would leave me alone. "I will do my best. I promise to do better."

"Well, I hope so. It's about time you take the next step in maturing."

I didn't respond and waited for him to exit my room. He stood there in the quiet awkwardness. I hoped he wouldn't ask me to look at him or something. I just wanted him to leave.

"I'll be leaving early Monday morning, more than likely before you wake up, so I'll be sure to say goodbye to you Sunday evening when you go to bed."

Wow, thank you for blessing me with your presence.

"Good to see you reading a book." He came closer and turned the front of the book. "I loved that story when I was a little lad."

That probably explained why I hated it.

"Well, I have to get out and run some errands. But I'll see you later for family dinner."

Family dinner. Every Saturday. No matter what. Even if my dad was gone, Mom and I would still have Saturday Family Dinner, and we seemed to have decent conversations. But when Dad happened to be home, dinner was usually stiffly silent. I wasn't looking forward to another Denner family dinner.

"Mom, see what Jay got us. He bought us some new clothes."

I could hear the delight in Jaiyde's voice when she greeted my mom at the door. I heard the rage in my mother, although she didn't speak a word. Then dense, long strides made their way toward the room Jaiyce and I shared. The no-knock warrant for raging moms materialized when the door blasted open. My mom's eye cocked up at me. Dread toppled my spirit.

"Why would you do that, Jayrin?"

"Do what?" I was sure what she was talking about, but I employed an ineffective stalling method.

"You know what! Why did you buy clothes for your brother and sister after I told you not to?"

"You told me not to get you anything, and I didn't."

"Boy, don't play games with me. You were well aware I didn't want you buying them anything either. And didn't you realize once they had those clothes, it would be difficult to pry anything from their hands? Now I have to be the bad guy." My memory couldn't conjure up a time when my mom was so furious with me.

"Or you could just let them keep it," I said. She twisted her head frantically.

"Jayrin, who are you? What in the hell has happened to you, Son? You truly think this is fine. You believe there's nothing wrong with selling drugs."

"I'm going to stop, Mom, okay," I said. "I promise. Just allow them to enjoy this stuff. You see how happy they are."

Quiet footsteps and ruffling plastic made their way towards the room. My mom and I turned and faced the door. Jaiyce shuffled in, dragging the two bags of clothes I had brought him. His steely eyes beamed into mine like a hawk. My insides startled. He dropped the sacks of clothes at the foot of my bed and walked out without uttering a peep.

My lips pursed, and I slowly lowered my head. In a flash, I realized I had failed my little brother. Though Jaiyce and Jaiyde knew their father, Devin, he wasn't really in their lives. They never went to his place. He would come over to visit them on their birthdays and some holidays.

When I was younger, Devin spent a lot of time at our apartment. I thirsted for a father, so I clung to his legs like a monkey on a tree branch. He didn't treat me like a son, but that didn't keep me from trying to be his son.

After Mom got pregnant, we moved from the small apartment to our small house, and Devin didn't come around as much, and after the twins were born, he came around even less. My vain attempts to find a father in Devin practically ended.

When my brother and sister grew older, it was clear Devin wouldn't be my stepfather. His relationship with Mom diminished, and Jaiyce and Jaiyde pretty much gave up on seeing him consistently.

Even though I never had the father I longed for, I somehow needed to be the father figure for Jaiyde, especially for Jaiyce. I needed to lead by example and keep an eye on Jaiyce to make sure he didn't go the same route I eventually inexplicably had traveled. However, the drop of the bags of clothes screamed failure. Jaiyce seemed aware that I had abandoned my post of being someone to follow and look up to.

We both lacked positive male role models, and Jaiyce looked to me to fill that void, which I did for a while.

Taking care of my siblings when my mom worked was necessary, and I took pride in doing so. I made sure they got their homework done, prepared their food, and ensured they did their chores. They expressed the appreciation they had for their big brother.

But lately, I deserted my responsibilities at home. Jaiyce's actions of dropping the bag epitomized my recent behavior. I dropped the ball. The devastation was a blow that struck me back to reality. It made me even more driven to hand over the gun and phones to Dymond, put my gear in reverse, and never look back.

****

I hit the spot around nine-fifteen. A blanket of blackest darkness covered the sky. The aroma of a crisp fall Saturday night filled the air. The bustling of rubber on the road, car horns, and hip-hop music vibrated from the adjacent streets. Dymond sat in anticipation. I greeted him with a fist bump. He greeted me with a grunt.

"What took you so long?" he asked.

"Just at the crib thinking."

"Thinking about what?"

"Something you said before. About how if your heart ain't in this, you might as well get out."

Dymond shot a look of surprise and disappointment at me. "That what you feeling? Thinking about getting out?"

"It crossed my mind," I said, trying to sound indecisive.

Dymond pursed his lips and turned his eyes up the street. "If that's what you on, go ahead and do it." He hesitated.

"After tonight, though. Once you receive your portion, you gotta sell it or pay for it yourself. Can't give dirty weed back to the boss, boss!"

Not what I wanted to hear. But I guess one more night couldn't hurt. Cars started arriving, blinking their headlights. A few of Dymond's regular customers came, and those who weren't, I took care of. After serving one car, I headed back across the street, but before I could get back over, a silver Kia Optima stopped and blinked. Dymond gave me a head nod instructing me that I could serve those customers.

I walked over to the car and counted three guys. All looked like older teenagers. All hooded up. After going through the progression of my routine, I stuck my hand inside, expecting money. What I got instead petrified me like nothing else. The driver snatched my arm, and the dude in the passenger seat promptly presented a gun and pointed it directly at my dome.

Frozen.

My eyes barely wandered to the back seat when I heard a voice. The back boasted dark gloominess but not dark enough for me to miss another dude with a gun. Throaty speech escaped his mouth. "Don't say a word." The pastiness in my mouth glued my lips shut. "Don't scream. Don't make a sound." My breathing became rapid, although I was sure I held my breath. I tried to swallow the pasty spit in my mouth but couldn't struggle the lump down my throat. The back seat spoke again.

"My man up there," he waved his offhand towards the driver, "is going to take everything out of your sleeves, and as soon as he's done, you gonna take the dope and money out of your pockets and hand it over to him. Try anything stupid, and you're inviting two bullets in your head before you can blink once."

My shaking hands barreled through my pockets with reckless abandon when I grappled the cold steel. The gun. Should I have pulled it out? No, that was a dumb idea—two guns against one. And the one, being me, had never fired a gun before. I grabbed bags from each of my front pockets along with around one hundred bucks. The snatch and run was over in seconds. The car peeled off, leaving the thumping in my chest in overdrive. My eyes caught Dymond. He stood up. I stood still.

"They robbed me," I said once I finally made it back over to the house. "Took my weed and my money."

"Dang man, you didn't pull out your piece on them jack boys?"

"Jack boys? What's that?" I asked, ignoring the fact that I didn't use the gun.

"Dudes who rob other dudes for their drugs and money. That's all they do. How much they get?"

"About a hundred dollars."

"How much of the stuff?"

"Six dimes, seven nickels." My body trembled like an earthquake. "Two dubs."

"Two hundred dollars worth of drugs and a hundred cash. Three hundred dollars total."

"Yeah."

"You know you gotta give the money back, right?"

"I do?"

"Yeah, and the money for the weed. I can vouch for you for a couple of days, but after that, you better have their money."

"How am I gon' do that?"

"You got some money at home, don't you?"

"No, I spent it all at the mall today."

Dymond sympathetically smacked his lips, rotating his head left and right. "That's all bad."

"What am I gon' do?" I asked desperately.

"Well, you better figure it out quick. They find out you got jacked and decided not to reimburse them, they will find you, and it won't be pretty," Dymond warned.

"They gon' kill me?" My eyes felt misty. I was positive Dymond thought I would cry. "For three hundred dollars?"

"They might not kill you right away, but they will come after you first, then scare your people if you don't pay the money back. After a few unsuccessful attempts, then they will probably off one of your family members before they do you." Dymond said that so calmly like it was an everyday occurrence.

"What? That's crazy. For a few hundred dollars?" I paused. "Man, what am I gonna do?"

"Might cop some items or money when we break into cars later."

I forgot about that. I was supposed to step out of the game that night. However, I had been robbed, and I needed to find a way to earn money back. I could have taken the clothes back. Then again, I couldn't; at least I couldn't take back Jaiyde's stuff. Especially after the fuss I made with my mother about the clothes. Taking Jaiyce's stuff back wouldn't have worked either because, after our talk, my mom gave him his clothes.

My biggest ticket item rested comfortably on my feet. I was sure the bottoms had dirt on them. The store wouldn't have taken them back at that point. So I guessed the only thing left for me to do was to go breaking into cars and sell more weed the following night again. Seemed to be my only option. I was so screwed!

"Hey, Dymond, can I borrow some money from you?"

He looked at me like I asked if I could borrow his liver or kidney.

****

I couldn't sleep because the two barrels from the guns in the Kia constantly stared at me when I closed my eyes. I was spooked like never before, and I willed my eyes to stay open.

Dymond's text vibrated my phone, and I flinched. Hurriedly, I snatched it up before it disturbed Jaiyce from his slumber.

Two-thirty-seven, according to the screen on the phone. My fingers responded to Dymond's text to come outside with an underwhelming 'k.' Jaiyce's heavy breathing mimicked snoring declaring him voluntarily unconscious, which allowed me to sneak out of our room undetected.

Outside, I hopped in a different car than the one Dymond had earlier. A Toyota Corolla. Somebody sat in the front seat. I slipped in the back. "What happened to your other car?"

"Fool, that wasn't my car."

"Well, how did you have it?"

"Why you asking so many questions?" asked the passenger.

"Who are you?" I tried to sound somewhat tough but didn't know how well it came off.

"That's Zyus. He gon' be walking and checking cars with you." I gave a fake head nod.

"Where he from?"

"Fool, I'm right here. You can ask me," Zyus barked. The agitation in the vehicle was roaring.

"Bro, why you all in your feelings?"

"I ain't yo bro, bro!" he said.

I threw my hands up in an *I give up* way and shook my head in disbelief.

"You little girls done cat-fighting? We got a long drive, and I don't want to hear this all the way out to the county."

"Whatever, man!" I retorted.

After a while, we arrived in a neighborhood which looked the exact opposite to mine. The houses were flawless. Not extremely huge, but perfectly shaped, clean-cut lawns, and nice cars in the driveways. Dymond instructed Zyus to take the cars on the right side and me on the left. Zyus hopped out, but I remained unsure of what I should do.

"Just go to each car and check the door handles. Doors that don't open means go on to the next car. If the door opens, go in, close the door quietly and go through the middle console, the glove compartment, and under the seat."

I opened the door. Dymond continued, "Take no more than thirty seconds and haul out. Take whatever can sell for twenty bucks or more. Of course, take any money, including coins. Shut the door gently and walk up the street to the next car. You hear me beep the horn twice, stop wherever you are, duck down, and wait until I beep the horn twice again before getting up."

"That's a lot to remember."

"A piece of cake. I'll be driving slowly. Be ready to jump in the car if something goes wrong."

"Something like what?" I asked.

"Like a car owner bursting out the house with a gun ready to bust." My body sat paralyzed, still visualizing the guns itching to bust at me six hours before. The thought reminded me why I was out there breaking into cars.

Getting robbed sucked.

Then I was the one robbing.

To be honest, that sucked too. But I did it. I opened car doors, rifled through the cars, took what I could, and repeated the process as we went through several blocks.

Two hours later, Zyus and I tumbled back in the car, hand and pockets full of stolen items. "What you cop, Jay?" I ran down the items I had, mostly pocket change. No wallets, no credit cards, no computers. I did find an old-looking iPod, though, and Dymond explained we'd take some stuff to some pawnshops, and we could sell some of it on the street. I doubted I had enough things to pay back the drugs and money I had lost. I definitely needed to sell more weed to make up for what I had lost. Dymond said doing this five times a week, could easily put an extra thousand dollars in my pocket each month.

"So tonight, we are only going to be out for a couple of hours, and then we hitting the club, boys," Dymond said.

I glanced up while putting items back into my pockets. "The club? On Sunday?"

"Yeah, a new joint in North County. Club Envy. I been there a few times. Eighteen and under. But tonight gon' be lit—Battle of the Bands night. Everybody knows University City

High School gonna win that, though. U. City got a band like one of them Black colleges. You know, like an HBCU or something."

"Historically Black Colleges and Universities," I chimed in.

"Yeah, one of those. I'm telling you, it's gonna be popping. So many chicks will be in the spot. And we can sell dope there too, of course," Dymond continued. "Should be able to make a gang of money. Them kids be feigning for it. Jay, you definitely need to make some more money to pay off your debt."

Unfortunately, he was right. I needed to get some money quickly so that I could get out of this game.

"Don't look so sad," Dymond teased. "You will have a lot of fun. Trust me."

I nodded in agreement, even though I didn't want to have a good time. I just wanted to be done with all of this.

CHAPTER 26 ~ Kamree

✱✱✱✱✱✱✱✱

I had to admit. I didn't focus during church. I had not been able to sleep the night before. I was too worried about Jayrin. He didn't call me or text me back after I made efforts to contact him. I told myself to just forget it, forget him; however, I couldn't stop thinking, wondering, and worrying. Even at three o'clock in the morning, I sat, anticipating my phone to light up. But it never happened. He didn't call, didn't text.

Finally, I reluctantly fell asleep for what seemed like thirty seconds before my mom started pounding on my door to wake me up for church. My world was disoriented, but I did muster the mental capacity to recheck my phone—still nothing. I checked Snapchat to see if anyone had posted anything about somebody getting killed or something. I tried to push the thought away, but it kept forcing its way into my mind.

Although rage engulfed me, my heart lingered tenderly on Jayrin, hoping he was okay, hoping nothing had happened to him. Saturday nights in our city continually proved to be a prime night for young black people to breathe their last breath. I desperately did not want Jayrin to be one of those statistics.

After a church service filled with me constantly checking my phone, I sat on my bed and attempted to complete my geometry homework, but my head pounded with a rhythmic hammering, swallowing my focus. I eventually put the book and pencil down and swiftly fell asleep. My ring tone aroused me out of my sleep and I blinked my eyes into focus to to find my phone.

"Where have you been?" I sounded groggy.

"Hello to you, too," he responded.

"No, no. Don't 'hello' me. I called and texted you all night, and it's," I looked at my screen, "almost four o'clock the next day, and you are just now calling me. Where have you been?"

"Do you not remember the last time we talked? You hung up on me? How could you expect me to come running back to you?"

"You can't answer the question. Is that because you don't want to tell me where you've been?"

"I don't need to answer you. I don't have to tell you everywhere I go. Remember, we aren't exactly going together, right?"

The surge of pain in my head raced through my entire body, but my energy level ignored the physical agony. I was past pissed off. Fury inflamed me. Jayrin infuriated me.

"You're right. Don't tell me where you were because I already know. With that fool, Dymond. All night? You told me you were going to tell him you were through with him. Yet, you stayed out till at least three in the morning, doing what? I thought you got robbed or hurt or something worse."

He hesitated. His following words punched me with an impactive blow.

"I don't have to tell you everything I'm doing. Who I'm with. Where I'm going. Hell, even if you were my girlfriend, that wouldn't be happening. Get off my case!"

"Get off your case?" I asked faintly. "Get off your case?" with more vigor. "You know what? I'm not only getting off your case; I'm getting off the phone. You go do you, Jayrin, and don't worry about me because I certainly won't be worrying about you." I calmed down ever so slightly, waiting for a response, but I heard none. I erupted once more. "Oh yeah, and don't think of me ever being your girlfriend because that won't be happening!"

I threw my phone on my plush pillow and started crying like a baby. Couldn't decide if I cried because I was sad or because I was mad.

Yeah, it was both.

With every tear that flowed, the pain in my head grew louder, and the pain in my heart violently ripped me apart.

CHAPTER 27 ~ Aceson

****

I returned to school for the first time in a week. While walking the hallways, I sensed numerous sets of eyeballs lasered in on me. The whispers hummed a little louder than typical as well. Part of me wanted to jump at anybody to make them flinch, but that was how I would respond before my suspension. The new me decided not to instigate situations and not to get in any trouble. I was determined to turn over a new leaf.

In my classes, reactions played out differently. Most kids occupied themselves too intensely with their school work to be concerned with me. Teachers weren't as snarky as their typical selves. The scenes suggested everyone ignoring me to the best of their abilities. It made me feel more like an outsider than usual. Well, I guessed going along with their neglect helped me stay out of troubling predicaments. After all, I never experienced positive interactions with anyone, anyway.

In the cafeteria, I sat at my usual table, alone, taking in the usual array of chatter from the room full of teenagers, who participated in a daily ritual of uncontrolled lunch vigor. I chomped at my sweaty pizza and just wanted the day to be over.

Then a kid I had never seen before stumbled to my table, tray in hand, glasses barely attached to his face. He fixed his gaze on me and placed his plastic tray on my table. I regarded him and wondered why he thought sitting at my table was a good idea. Obviously, he didn't know me. I felt it necessary to make him aware of who I was.

But, I forgot, I had committed to being a different Aceson. I needed to do this the right way. I needed to let him down gently when assuring him that he couldn't sit with me. It was my table, and I always sat by myself, mainly because no one wanted to sit with me.

"Hey, kid, what are you doing?" I asked as nicely as possible.

"I'm sitting down to eat my lunch."

"You sure you want to sit here?"

"Of course, I do," he responded calmly.

"I don't think you do. You see, no one sits with me."

The boy adjusted his glasses and sat down as if I had said nothing to him. My head tilted slightly, and I scratched my temple, eyes squinted.

"Yep, I was right. You must be the infamous Aceson Denner," he said, right before stuffing his face with a forkful of lettuce.

"How did you know my name?"

"Easy. Deductive reasoning. I didn't see you here last week. Students talked about you each day, saying how much they delighted in your five days out of school. You were the only kid in the cafeteria sitting by himself today, which demonstrated no one was interested in enjoying your company. Oh, and yeah, you tried your best to keep me away. Maybe because you wanted to show what a bully you've always been, or maybe because you are comfortable being lonely."

"Who are you, Dr. Phil or somebody?" My blood started boiling. "You don't know me!"

"Oh, so you like sitting by yourself?"

"Yes, I mean no. I mean... well, people just treat me like an outcast. You have no idea what that's like." Just as soon as those words escaped my mouth, I tried to suck them back in but realized it too late. "I'm sorry. I didn't... I mean... I."

"This is the second school I've been to this year. And we are only in November. The third school since seventh grade. All Catholic schools, and in each one, I happened to be one of only a handful of Black students. When I arrived here last week, nobody knew me. No one knew if I was mean or nice, and no one took the time to find out. No one told me that you were a jerk; I heard it as kids conversed with one another; not one student spoke directly to me."

He took a bite of his greasy pizza and slugged down milk. My body sat still. This kid communicated coolly yet with authority.

"I was the only one sitting at this table last week. No one attempted to sit with me or to invite me to their table for four straight days. It doesn't matter. I'm used to it. Like I said, three schools since last year, and it's been the same at each one."

"Well, I don't want to sound rude or anything, but did you ever try to initiate friendships?"

"I think I'm doing that with you now," he replied.

"Oh."

A tinge of shame and contentment saturated through me.

CHAPTER 28 ~ Jayrin

✱✱✱✱✱✱✱✱

My head boomed from lack of sleep and the crazy time I had at the club the previous night. I saw another side of Dymond. He always seemed to be all business, but after selling his product to a bunch of kids there, Dymond smoked some weed and drank some beer himself. I had no idea! I had no idea that they allowed teenagers to drink and smoke in a club. I tried some drink, and even though I didn't actually like it, I kept going at it. I refused to be the only lame in the place. It was crazy. It was wild. It was loud.

Once I woke up, it took me forever to gain my bearings. In the bathroom, I viewed myself in the mirror. My disheveled hair echoed an incomplete bird's nest. My eyes were pink balloons with dark dots in the middle. An angry headache beat my head like a drum, and I absolutely didn't want to go to school. Of course, I knew I wouldn't stay at school the entire day, but the morning classes would murder me.

I splashed water on my face, brushed my teeth, and willed myself to put on clothes. I remembered talking to that girl, Lexiah, at the club, and we kinda hit it off. The thought of seeing her at school aroused me to flee the house as soon as possible. I didn't eat anything for breakfast, dressed in my new clothes and my new Jordans, and shot out the door without saying anything to my mom. I didn't know if she realized I was out past two in the morning again, and I didn't want to hear it.

During my twenty-five-minute walk to school, my head was in the clouds despite the headache. The feeling of being hip with my fresh clothes and Jordans on my feet was a new vibe. And having a chick like Lexiah on me was a bonus. I felt like I had some for real clout.

Overnight I went from this scared, little kid who got robbed and determined to give up the opportunity to make money to a baller, ready to make more money, hook up with a bad chick, and never get robbed again. If somebody tried, they would have another thing coming.

During my first hour class, I think I fell asleep a total of four times. Mrs. Underwood, my history teacher, tapped my desk three times to get me up, but she obviously gave up because the bell rang and shook me from my slumber instead of Mrs. Underwood. I wiped the slobber from my cheeks, and I headed straight for the door when Mrs. Underwood stopped me.

"You're forgetting your map and timeline, Jayrin," she said.

"What you talking about?"

"Your homework. The map and timeline of American history: 1920-1944. It's what we discussed in class today. Oh, I'm sorry, I overlooked the fact that you decided to take your morning nap in class today. How could I be so inconsiderate?"

Mrs. Underwood had two appropriate nicknames: Mrs. Thunderwood or Mrs. Underwear, depending on what she wore. Thunderwood, if she dressed in her fluffy skirt with flowers exposing her tree trunk thighs; Underwear if she wore her black yoga pants displaying her granny panties lines that received more stank-face grimaces than laughs. We didn't concoct a clever nickname for her when she bravely wore mom jeans that helped exhibit her bowling ball gut.

Mrs. Underwood was also sarcastic, which I couldn't understand for the life of me. Why would someone who dressed and looked the way she did think that she could be sarcastic to a group of high school students? She had to realize we talked about her, didn't she? "Oh, I forgot," I said, walking back to the table, grabbing the pieces of paper.

"Of course, if your mother had bought you a Chromebook rather than those expensive-looking shoes, you could access the work online." I bowed my head at my J's.

"My mom didn't buy these," I grunted as I made my way to the door again.

"Oh, really!" She sounded surprised. "Well, who purchased them for you?"

"I bought them myself," I said as I spilled out into the hall, headed for my locker.

When I arrived at the locker, Lexiah stood, waiting for me. Short and thick, red lips, and long eyelashes. I mean, she always appeared beautiful to me, but I never gave her a second thought because she never gave me a first thought. But since last night, things may have changed. "What's up, Jay?" Dang, her voice was smooth and sexy.

"Lexi! What's up with you?" My fingers spun my combination lock. My stomach was turning too. My nerves were hidden by my sudden bravado.

"Nothing much, just glad to see you."

"No doubt, girl."

"I had so much fun last night," she said.

I didn't know where I mustered up the sauce to talk to her because she made me nervous, but for some reason, I had glided through our conversations the night before at the club.

"Yeah, I was digging it too. You're cool to be with. We should hang out more," I said.

"Oh, for sure. What you doing this weekend?"

"Nothing for real. What you wanna do?"

"How about the mall?"

"Yeah, we can do that."

"Cool." She glanced up and down the crowded hallway. "Well, I guess we should go to class."

"Yeah, I guess you right. Let's sit together in the cafeteria at lunch," I said. I shoved the now crumpled history homework paper into my locker.

"Sure, I'd love to."

"Cool, cool."

I was about to slam the locker shut when she stuck her manicured hand on the door.

"Don't you have something for me?"

I told her at the club that I would bring a surprise for her. I peeked inside the locker and spotted the bag I brought to school with me. I took it out and handed it to her. She reached out, grabbed it, and gave me a peck on my cheek before trotting off. My body stood still for a second, and I processed what had just happened.

Then I beamed from cheek to cheek.

New week. Fresh start. My new motto.

After telling Jayrin off Sunday and letting him know I was done with him, I once again vowed to concentrate on my studies more than fixating on a boy. Although I didn't receive anything spiritual at church, because I occupied my mind on Jayrin, I realized I should focus on God and doing what's right in His eyes instead of focusing on anybody else.

My renewed focus proved to be exactly what I needed. Even though I had not been struggling in my academics, my mind started to move in a different direction. As necessary as having friends could be, I had to realize there were more important things to hold on to. I loved Kaprina, but Kaprina loved herself more than anything or anyone else. I thought I loved Jayrin despite the fact I hated what he was doing and who he had become. Shifting my mindset helped me take control of who I was and who I was becoming.

I understood, however, my quest would be an uphill battle, especially after experiencing the scene in the cafeteria at lunch. Jayrin sat with Lexiah Lewis. When did they become cool like that? He stayed for the entire lunch period. Didn't leave and go to his *'spot'* like he does every other day. And worse, witnessing what Lexiah wore. A cropped camo jacket with a frayed bottom! I couldn't believe this. Wearing my... probably the jacket Jayrin said he bought for me? The one I refused to accept. Why did I feel a certain way about this? A slap in the face and betrayal to the highest degree. How could Jayrin do this?

To me?

I needed to go say something to him. Advise him about Lexiah being a thirsty little gold-digger. Warn him that hanging out with her would break him. Inform him she was Kaprina's enemy; translation: she was my enemy.

Wait. Why did I do this to myself? Jayrin couldn't care less about any of this. I told him I no longer wanted to be with him, which meant he was probably done with me too. Why did I have so much concern? This ridiculous tug-of-war pulled me in both directions, straining me.

I cared so much because I had known Jayrin for nearly ten years—I met him at age five when we started kindergarten. I cared because as a Black male living in a city where Black males were vulnerable to untimely deaths, his new life would take him out early. I cared because Jay was my friend. Unfortunately, though, probably my friend no more.

"Dang, girl. Why you let that boy get to you?" Kaprina shook me out of my mental trance. I twisted my head at her. "Lunch is about over, and you haven't eaten anything."
I looked down at my lunch tray. Full and untouched. "Guess I wasn't hungry," I said.

"So, that's what it is," Kaprina said, with little assurance.

Before school, I told Prina what had happened over the weekend with Jayrin. Her words from before really rang true: *It's wrong to be looking for Mr. Right. He'll always be Mr. Wrong...* I never knew whether to take Kaprina seriously or not. She seemed to possess good mature wisdom mixed with immature hood values and virtues.

Her personality reflected our relationship: she said dumb stuff, which made a lot of sense; she did things to gain attention but didn't think about what other people thought of her; she often ignored me but always came to my rescue whenever I needed it.

"Hey, is that the jacket you told me about? The one Jayrin got for you?" Jayrin and Lexiah walked toward the wastebasket and dumped their trash from their trays.

"I don't know. Never saw the jacket."

"Yep, she wearing your jacket. I should go over there and snatch the thing off the little skank. She always trying to hook up with somebody for their money." I think Prina didn't like Lexia because they acted just the same.

"You don't have to. I don't want the stupid jacket," I admitted.

"I'm not talking about getting the jacket for you. I'm trying to get it for me. Did you see that thing? The jacket is dope! With them ripped jeans and black boots, her fit is pretty legit. For real, for real."

I shook my head.

After a successful first day back in school without getting into any trouble, I readied myself for an even better second day. Classmates treated me the same, ignoring me. Teachers again had nothing positive to say to me. Whispers again echoed in the hallways. I got through it without a blemish. Then at lunch, the kid from the previous day was at my table. He was already engaged in his spaghetti, head down, glasses sliding off his face.

"How are you today, Aceson?" he said without looking up at me.

"I'm okay. How are you?" I realized I didn't know his name.

"I'm fine."

I put my tray on the table. "So, what's your name, anyway?"

"Izaiah, with a z. Izaiah Parnell."

"What school were you at before coming here?"

"We lived in Indiana. I went to a school called Reformation Catholic. Wasn't as becoming as this one."
He slurped some spaghetti from his utensil. The usual slimy pizza slice was in the clutch of my hand.

"This school is okay," I said. "But I'd rather be somewhere else. Students here are so privileged. They think they're supposed to get anything they want." My eyes made their way around the cafeteria surroundings. Clean white walls. Colorful drapes. New tables. An assembly of rich kids enveloped in shallow conversations about superficial topics. "How are you able to afford this school," I asked. Izaiah's fork stopped mid-air, mouth opened, eyes shifted from his food to me.

"What do you mean?" he replied.

"I mean, what kind of work do your parents do to afford this school. It's expensive."

"Really?" he asked bitterly. "Well, my dad is a captain in the Air Force and works at Scott Air Base across the river in Illinois, and my mom is a professor at Washington University." He took another bite and then scrolled his eyes up to me. "How can *you* afford to go to this school?"

My forehead wrinkled. I didn't know how to answer the question after putting the proverbial foot in my mouth the day before. But I took it out of my mouth to break the muted moment. "My dad owns a financial business, and my mom is a secretary at a high school in the city." He showed no emotion, just kept chewing. I took a bite myself, not knowing what else to say.

So, of course, I seasoned my big toe, stuck it in my mouth once again, and began speaking. "I wish I could go to the school where my mom works, but they won't let me because the school is for poor kids, and they say my parents make too much money, mostly my dad, though." I stuck my fork in my mouth so I could take my foot out and shut up. Geez, why did I say that?

He chuckled slightly. "That sucks."

Moments of silence followed. Then, out of the blue, Izaiah asked me a question I didn't expect. "So, you want to be friends?"

He was nonchalant. Thoughts swirled through my mind, but an answer didn't easily flow from my mouth. And finally, I responded slowly. "I don't know." Izaiah looked up at me and adjusted the glasses on his nose. Confusion covered his face. "I've never had a Black friend before. I haven't had many friends at all. None since I started middle school, but I don't know if I can be a friend with a Black person," I said.

His eyes went back down to his tray of food. I sensed his disappointment. "It's not that I'm prejudiced or anything, it's just I don't think we have anything in common. Things you like, I probably don't like."

The ding of the lunch bell rang, and students began heading to exit the cafeteria. Izaiah remained silent and calm, dumped his trash in the can, and walked out. I obviously said some dumb things again, but luckily I was saved by the bell.

I asked Monae to take me to get a driver's permit. She told me to bring my birth certificate and proof of address, so I snuck into Mom's room. She kept them in her drawer with important papers, and I had to make sure to put them back as soon as possible before she noticed they were missing.

At school, I sat next to Lexiah again in the cafeteria. She talked about how excited she was to go to the mall. That was the main reason I wanted my permit. I planned to ask Dymond to drive his car. But I also needed to ask him to teach me how to drive before then. He also promised to show me how to shoot a gun so I'd be ready for anyone who tried to jack me for my money or weed again.

Kamree appeared to be distraught while sitting at her lunch table. Not sure why, but maybe she regretted kicking me to the curb and hated seeing me with Lexiah. Jealousy didn't look good on her.

She walked over toward us but stopped, turned around, and stomped out of the cafeteria. For some strange reason, I wished Kamree had confronted me and Lexiah to fight for me. Two girls fighting over me after going my entire life without having a girl would have been huge.

My reputation had changed seemingly overnight because of the new drip I wore and because a popular girl was sitting with me. To drive would be the icing on the cake. There'd be nothing anyone could say to me. Clothes, girls, cars. Those would make me one of the freshes freshmen in the school.

After lunch, I left and sat on Monae's porch for a couple of hours, selling weed until she came out to tell me we were going. Minutes later, she backed out of her shabby garage, white with chipped paint all over, in a 2018 pearl white Mercedes Benz. My jaw dropped. How did someone who lived in a dilapidated house drive such an immaculate car?

The Benz hummed down the driveway and stopped, waiting for me to plop inside. Brown leather seats and wood grain interior made for a pretty inside that equaled the outside of the ride. I had never been in a car so impressive. There were many Benz pictures in my room from magazines. It was probably my favorite car. Perhaps one day, I would have one.

Driving to the Department of Motor Vehicle office was a quiet ride. The only thing Monae said to me was when she asked if I had read the study booklet she had given me. I told her I had, and I pulled it out of my backpack and skimmed through it for the remainder of the drive for some last-minute cramming.

At the DMV office, my hand trembled when handing the paperwork to the woman behind the Plexiglas. I figured she would determine Monae wasn't my mother, considering how young she looked. I didn't know how old Monae was, and I had no clue about her last name. To my surprise, the transaction went fine. I passed the test with an eighty percent and walked out with my paper permit in less than an hour.

The ride back again remained muted until I decided to ask Monae a stupid question. "Can you teach me how to drive? I would love to whip this car."

"Boy, you crazy? You ain't getting in this car again."

Oh, well, that was quite blunt.

"Can I ask you something else?"

"No," she snapped.

I wondered how she afforded that car. I never saw her

sell any drugs. What did she do to earn her money? Did she keep all the money we put in her mailbox?

"Can you take me driving?" I asked Dymond when Monae and I returned to the house.

"Yeah, but you know I'm not legally able to take you. I don't have my license."

"But you be driving your cars without a license."

Dymond peered at me, scratched his head, and chuckled. "You really think those be my cars?"

"Yeah. Aren't they?"

"Fool, I be jacking those whips. Whenever I need to go somewhere, I go to a parking lot or walk up on somebody's driveway, pull out my piece, and carjack 'em. You think I'm gonna have my own car at fifteen?"

Stupidity reigned in my mind as I thought about what Dymond had said. "So, I guess I can't ask to use one of the cars you jacked to take Lexiah to the mall this weekend?"

"You wanna drive, you gotta steal your own car. I can tell you the best spots to go cop one."

The thought of pulling out a gun to rob somebody of their car was not what I had in mind. Thinking about those guns pointed at my face a few days ago gave me the chills, made me cold but made me not want to take something by force from an unsuspecting person.

Sure, I wanted some revenge on those dudes who had robbed me, and I would be willing to go after anyone who came after me, but pointing a piece at some old lady or an innocent kid who had just started driving was a horrible thing to think.

"You ain't up to it, are you?"

"If that's what I gotta do, I will," I said, half meaning it.

CHAPTER 32 ~ Kamree

✱✱✱✱✱✱✱✱✱

I couldn't take it anymore. I needed to warn Jayrin about Lexiah. Things he was doing worked my nerves, but I didn't want to see him get hurt. Lexiah's way of doing things consisted of getting whatever she could and hurting whoever got in the way in the process. Jayrin happened to be that somebody in the way, and he would get run over by the wicked witch of the Midwest.

So, I hopped up to give her a piece of my mind. Then I thought about how Jayrin had been treating me lately and figured he might take her side and make me look silly. My feet stopped dead, spun me around, and I stomped right out of the cafeteria. I headed to my favorite spot to throw myself a pity party.

A few minutes later, the creak of the door startled me. A few seconds later, Prina opened the stall door to find me sitting on the toilet. "I'm glad I was just sitting on this toilet and not actually doing something," I said.

"Whatevs. What you in here for now? You still trippin' off that boy?"

"Jayrin? Yes."

"Are you sure you should have been trying to get with him in the first place? I mean, you had just broken up with Travathian, and in no time, you were already thinking about getting with Jayrin. Like all of a sudden, you made your move. That's just not like you, Kam."

"But when I told you, you were all for it. Giving me props. Now you're questioning my decision?"

"You know I was trying to be in your corner. How would

it have looked for me to tell you it wasn't a good idea?"

"So, you didn't think he was good for me in the first place?"

"No, it just felt like you were rushing into it."

"Yeah, I guess you're right."

"Well, why did you let Jayrin go anyway?"

"I told you how much I hate that my father went to prison because he wanted to sell drugs, rob stores, and put his life of crime before his family. I haven't seen him since I was about four or five years old. If it wasn't for my stepfather taking me in and loving me like his own child from the beginning and helping me and my mom, I don't know where we'd be." For some reason, I wasn't in a hurry to get out of the bathroom stall this time. "He's the one who helped us understand our need to give our hearts to God and things turned around in our lives. Jayrin started acting more like my daddy instead of my stepfather."

"So, you think Jayrin gonna grow up to be like your daddy?" I shrugged my shoulders. "You can't predict Jayrin's future. You went through the same thing with Travathian, leaving him because of something he did in the past. You won't find the perfect person, Kam. You have to learn to forgive and move on. Ain't that what your God wants you to do?"

Again, Kaprina was always good for saying something so profound, even when she didn't live out what she was speaking. Her words made me take a look in the mirror and reflect on how I treated people who weren't exactly what I wanted them to be.

"Has your stepfather always been perfect?"

"I guess not."

"No, he hasn't, because nobody is, and you accepted him

because his imperfections are different from your father's. You know I ain't into church like you, but I am sure of one thing; sin is sin. And if God can forgive people, certainly you can."

Dang, she was right. Maybe I should fight for Jayrin instead of watching him spin out of control. That would be the right thing to do whether he was my boyfriend or not.

"Kam, you know I love you girl. But for real, you need to think about what you be doing. Low-key, not too many people here like you." That's really high-key—I kind of already knew that. "The girls I be hanging with. They think you stuck up. They don't know you like I do. I know you mean well, but sometimes, you give people a bad impression."

I felt like Prina was taking the hand of those girls and hitting me in the gut with them. "I don't mean anything by it. I'm just trying to do what I think is best. What's best for me."

Prina huffed. "Everything ain't always going to work out for the best. Sometimes you just gotta live and let other people live. You are fifteen years old, and you trying to be forty-five. Be a kid. Have fun."

"What do you mean?" I asked in distress.

"You do stuff that can be irritating."

"Like what?"

"Like thinking that everybody in the world gotta be perfect. Like every problem gotta be solved. Like the way you talk."

"What's wrong with the way I speak?"

"You talk White, all proper and stuff. Even your texts be written out with correct grammar. You don't use abbreviations, always got a period at the end of your sentences, always capitalizing stuff. Who does that?"

I squinched up my face. "Talk White? What does that even mean? And what's wrong with me wanting to use perfect English?"

"Cause, once again, ain't nobody perfect. So, stop trying to be."

"Well, forgive me for wanting to make something of myself. For wanting to prepare myself for college, get a couple of degrees, get a good job, and get out of this hellhole of a city."

Prina's mouth stood open. "Kam, did you just say 'hell' or do my ears deceive me?"

I calmed for a second. "Yes, I did."

"Does that mean you going to hell?"

I hesitated. "That's stupid. Of course not."

"See. Sometimes you can say something out of anger or do something that might not be the perfect thing to do, but that doesn't mean it's the end of the world."

Knowing that my crazy, carefree friend was always good for making sense out of nonsense, I sighed.

"Yeah, I guess you're right."

The last few days had been a total bummer at school. I felt terrible all week because of the horrible things I said to Izaiah, and he hadn't spoken to me since Tuesday. He sat at a different table by himself during lunch, which meant I sat by myself too.

A couple of days ago, I tried to speak to my mom about the issue, but I couldn't gather the courage considering how I had treated Izaiah. She would be disappointed in me. Again. She, however, proved to be easier to talk to than my dad. She listened to me. She heard my side of the story. She always attempted to get my dad to go easy on me whenever I messed up.

A part of me thought she might understand. I mean, heck, we just didn't associate with Black people. We weren't racists or anything. All the schools I'd gone to had very few or no Black kids at all. No Black people attended our church, and the street we lived on had one inter-racial family who moved out a couple of years ago. The most I understood about African Americans developed from what I saw on television. Since they were actors, those probably weren't the best representations.

So, who could blame me for feeling disconnected from Izaiah? For not knowing how to talk to him, how to be his friend? It was not that I didn't want to be his friend. I didn't think I could be his friend. I didn't believe I could do the things he liked or say the things he wanted to hear.

Honestly, I didn't know how to be anyone's friend, seeing I had never had any real friends anyway. See, it had nothing to do with him being Black at all. And with this newfound information, I convinced myself to walk over to the table where he sat.

Tray in hand, I strolled over. He perched at one of the smaller round tables—not one of the longer rectangle ones we had been sitting at together. My tray dropped on the table, and I plopped down on the stool across from him. He didn't even look up; he continued eating lettuce from his salad like I didn't exist. Like I was invisible.

Maybe it was a favorable sign he didn't get up and walk away. Butterflies crowded my stomach, and I feared taking a bite of my slimy pizza. Eventually, I chucked out a few words. "I'm sorry for what I said to you the other day. After thinking about it, I realized I do want to be your friend." He kept his head bowed down to his food. He didn't flinch. "Really, man, I think you would be a good friend. My best friend. The best friend I ever had." More like the only friend I ever had. "I said some stupid things the other day, and I hope you can forgive me."

"I forgive you," he said, but he continued eyeballing his plate of food, "but don't worry about being friends."

That was a punch in the gut. I couldn't believe what he had said. He started the whole *'let's be friends'* stuff in the first place, and then he changed *his* mind. "What do you mean? Why did you say that?"

"Because you already revealed how you feel about it. What's in your heart will always come out of your mouth. So, it's okay. I'm used to it."

Those words infuriated me. How was this little punk gonna diss me? How dare him. "But I don't understand. I'm telling you I do want to be your friend. I'm sorry for what I said before. I was wrong, and I'm admitting I was wrong. Why are you turning on me so easily?"

"Wasn't it easy for you to turn on me?" he asked.

"Yeah, but that was then, and I like I said, I was wrong. I don't understand why you won't forgive me for what I said and just move on."

"I said I forgive you, but I don't think I can forget what you said. *They* told us to move on for so long in this country. Act like those things never happened and do what ya'll want us to do. Usually, they end with, *'I can't be responsible for what my ancestors did to your ancestors hundreds of years ago.'* However, in this case, it's not what your ancestors did hundreds of years ago, but what you said a couple of days ago."

"What are you, a mini militant or something? Why are you bringing up your ancestors and all that?"

"I read, I research, and I study. My dad talks to me about history all the time. He loves it, and so do I," he responded. "That's why he joined the military in the first place.

He wanted to be part of history, wanted to make a positive contribution."

"So, you spend a lot of time with your father?"

"Of course. My dad's like my best friend. Even though he encourages me to find other friends, he understands making friends is difficult for me, and he enjoys being my padre and my compadre."

I wrestled with jealousy erupting in me.

Izaiah gobbled a little more of his food, stood, and shuffled over to the wastebasket where he dumped his partially eaten lunch. I ate nothing, but that didn't keep me from following his footsteps and tossing my food in the trash. I tried to hurry to catch up with him, but by the time I finished, he had vanished.

I desperately wanted to talk to him again to give him a piece of my mind. But I realized that it was not the best thing to do. I swallowed the fact that I missed out on possibly my only chance of having a real friend.

As usual, I couldn't do anything right!

✱✱✳✱✱✳✳✳

They called me to the office while I was sitting in second-hour science class. The secretary asked me to sit in the office waiting room until the principal finished his meeting. She said I was there to discuss my school attendance. It seemed booty backward for them to pull me out of class to tell me I was missing too many classes. Oh well, whatever.

The secretary was kinda freaking me out, though. The chick kept looking at me like I was gonna rob her or something. I tried to play it off like I was interested in the pictures and plaques on the walls, but out of my peripheral vision, I saw her staring. The crazy thing was, whenever I turned and looked at her, she kept eyeballing me. Most people would play it off and act like they were doing something else or looking at something else. But she didn't even try to fake it.

Maybe she was digging me, but I wasn't sure. She didn't appear to be too old, and yeah, she was cute for a White woman with her long dark hair and bronze tan.

A door opened and broke me out of my thoughts. A man and a woman walked out, whispering something. The man, the principal, looked at me and stopped. The woman—I had no idea who she was—didn't look at me but stopped at the desk and spoke to my new crush.

Principal Watkins, a burly White man, cleaned-shaven, with a balding hair island, considered me. I finally turned entirely toward him, and he spoke. "Mr. Foster, could you follow me, please?"

It was a question, so I wondered if I could've said no, but I didn't. But I wanted to. I pulled myself out of the chair, blew out a disrespectful breath, peeked at my new-found infatuation once more, and followed Principal Watkins.

Just as I entered his office, someone snuck up from behind me and closed the door. It was somewhat startling. "Take a seat, Mr. Foster," insisted Watkins, as he waved his hand at the chair in front of his desk. He sat in an oversized leather chair behind his desk, and the lady who was with him moments ago sat on a small sofa to the right of us. "This is Dr. Meadows, our school social worker."

"Hello, Jayrin," she said as she flipped open her spiral notebook, the kind with the rings at the top.

I hesitated, wondering why she knew my name, even though I had never seen this lady before in my life. "Hey," I grumbled.

"So, Jayrin, I'm going to get right to it," Watkins said. The social worker wrote something on her pad. He continued, "We probably should have brought you in sooner. Do you understand, though, that you have cut your afternoon courses almost every day for close to a month?"

My fingernail scratched my right cheek. No, the other right cheek. The one on my face. It was a stalling tactic. I wasn't sure if he wanted me to answer or not, but I did. "Nah, I haven't been keeping track."

"We've already had a conversation with your mother, and sadly, things have not changed. Can I ask why you've cut so many classes?"

"Yeah, you can ask." A moment of silence. He made a dumbfounded face with his hands in front of him, palms up. "Oh, you were asking, huh?" I said.

"Yes, I was."

"I got an afternoon job."

"Where?"

"That's personal."

He huffed. "You do understand it is against state mandates for a fifteen-year-old to work weekdays during school hours? No real establishment will risk hiring someone like you with the chance of losing their business license under the child labor laws."

"Sounds like that's not my problem." The doctor had been writing in her notebook the entire time.

"Well, unfortunately, we will need to involve the local authorities. Before we do, though, Dr. Meadows has few questions for you," Mr. Watkins said.

I turned toward her. She seemed to write quickly to finish up before speaking to me. "Jayrin, it's the educational responsibility for schools to provide a safe and rigorous learning environment, and it is your responsibility to be present to receive that education. Your parent or guardian must make sure you are coming to school. Otherwise, we, you, and your guardian are all out of compliance."

She continued, "You need to be in school a determinant number of hours each day and a certain number of hours for the school year. You must be present in school at least ninety percent of the total time possible. Your attendance is currently over ninety percent. However, your total hours of attendance is sixty-eight percent." She paused, glanced at the principal, and slightly bit her bottom lip. "Being absent more days, even if they are half days, will only bring those numbers down even more and further extend the gap between your attendance and the appropriate amount."

"Okay, and you're telling me all of this because?"

"Because we've previously given this information to your mother. Now, we are giving it to you. You heard of the adage, *Three strikes, and you're out*? Well, this is your second strike. If we have to speak to you and your mother once more, that will be your third strike, and we will treat this as a truancy case." She exerted a weighty face. "Do you understand what truancy is, Jayrin?"

"Nah, not really." My mom did tell me something about it, but I didn't really get it.

"It means with so many unexcused absences, your mother can be called to attend truancy court and could be fined up to twenty-five dollars for each day of school missed. Now, can she afford to take off work to show up at a courthouse for a hearing? Does she have the means to hire an attorney? Can she accumulate enough money to pay fines for something you're doing? Or not doing in this case?"

"Doubt it, but I can pay those fines myself. No big deal."

Dr. Meadows and Principal Watkins turned toward each other, and both sighed. Watkins spoke up. "This is not a game, Jayrin. I have no idea where you could be working, and I don't understand where you are getting your money from, but the decisions you're making are not just affecting you—"

The office phone rang, interrupting the speech. Watkins held out his index finger in a *hold that thought* manner. After picking up the phone, he nodded and said, "Thanks, send him in." He put the receiver down and stood.

Seconds later, the door opened, and the receptionist appeared. Now that she was from behind her desk, I got a good look at her body. I could tell that she worked out. Her arms and legs under her skirt were toned and athletic. She ushered a tall, muscular Black man inside. As she shut the door, she shot me another stare that lingered until the door was fully closed.

Creepy or freaky.

The man sat down in the spot formerly occupied by Dr. Meadows. She and Principal Watkins walked toward the door. Confusion swirled through my mind. Principal Watkins whispered something in the man's ear.

"Hey, what's going on?" I said.

"This is Officer Nazarus Johnson. He's from the juvenile facility downtown. He's going to speak to you for a few minutes," Watkins said.

I turned up my nose at the officer. "I ain't got nothing to say to him, and I don't want to hear nothing he got to say either."

"Well, there's no choice, Jayrin," the man said.

"Well, I also have the right to remain silent, Officer Whatever," I said.

He chuckled. "You're not under arrest. And you can call me Officer Naz."

At that point, Watkins and Meadows had walked out of the office.

I sat in the office alone with a man I was unfamiliar with, a man I didn't want to talk to, and who I didn't want talking to me. I slumped in my chair and admired the ceiling.

"So, from what we have been able to detect, you had a clean record in middle school; a decent grade point average, advanced in most of your courses, pristine attendance," Officer Johnson said. "You've not done so well so far in high school. Any particular reason why?" He sat on the brown leather couch next to me.

"Not that I know of," I retorted.

"So, I hear you got yourself a job somewhere." He scratched his nose. I said nothing. "I see it all the time," he said, "good kids from the hood get tired of always doing the right thing, and tire of not having much and find other ways that are not exactly legal. Are you selling narcotics, Jayrin?"

"Selling drugs? Ha!"

"So, I guess I should take that as a yes?"

"You can take it how you want, Mr. Junior Officer."

"Okay, Mr. Tough Guy. You have no clue what you're getting yourself into. There are usually only two places this will lead you: jail or the grave," he said. "That's a cell or hell; heaven if you right with God."

I licked my lips and exhaled a gust of air. "I'm good on both of those," I said. "Can I go to class now?"

"I'll be having my eye on you. But in the meanwhile, if you ever come to your senses and need somebody to talk to, I'll be available for you." He stood, pulled out a wallet or something, and handed me a card. "My number is on there. You can call me anytime." I rolled my eyes. "I mean it, Jayrin," he said. "I know I come off as some tough guy myself, but really, I have a real soft spot when it comes to young brothers like you. Even though I work in the system, my mission in life is to keep kids out of the system. I don't want you to go down that path, just like I don't want anybody else to. That's why I do what I do."

He waited for a beat before continuing.

"I care."

I stood, took the card, barely scanned it, and put it in my back pocket, turned, and walked out of the room, passing through the main office where the secretary gawked at me once again. Principal Watkins and Dr. Meadows were talking at a table. Their voices retreated while I walked through the office, and their eyes beamed at me. I exited into the hallway and headed back to second hour.

CHAPTER 35 ~ Kamree

"Miss Covington, I would like you to run an errand for me," Mrs. Philby said near the end of my second hour class.

I pulled my eyes from my desk and turned my math paper over while looking at dirty stares from a few students. It was widely known I was the teacher's pet in all of my classes. I unashamedly did not shy away from the title. "Please take this envelope to the office and give it to the secretary." She handed me the envelope, and I walked out.

I arrived at the office, and I noticed Jayrin walking out. I had not spoken to him since I canceled him from my life. His being there caught me off guard, and I had no idea what to say. I wondered if I should say anything. The scene manifested in slow motion. Jayrin stood still as a statue when we made eye contact. I unintentionally crumbled the envelope between my fingers. The awkward moment forced my mouth open. "Jayrin?" I didn't understand why the word came out as a question. "Hey, how are you doing?" My tone was soft.

"I'm good."

He didn't ask me how I was doing, which disappointed me, but I didn't show it. "So, you are coming from the office. Everything alright?"

"Yeah, just talking to me about my attendance, that's all."

I peered at the envelope and realized it was crinkled. I tried to iron the paper out with my hands. "So, I've wanted to talk to you about something." He stared at me, dumbfounded. I glanced around and made sure no one else was in the hall listening to our conversation. "I want to speak to you about

Lexiah."

"Yeah, what about her?"

"Well, I guess you're kinda dating her or whatever."

"And?"

"And I wanted to make sure you knew something about her." His emotionless eyes stayed fixed on me. "You are aware she has a reputation of messing with dudes for their money?"

"Oh, really?" he asked.

"Yeah," I said.

"Well, I don't know nothing about that."

"How can you not see it? She only dates older guys with jobs or who sell drugs." I stopped and let it sink in. It didn't seem to work. "When you had no money, you didn't even exist to her."

"Whatever. I guess you jealous, huh? You still want me, don't you?"

"Oh no, I don't want you anymore. I still care about you, though, and I don't want you to get hurt." He started walking away.

"You ain't gotta worry about me."

"Jayrin, what happened to you? You've changed."

He stopped in his tracks. "Changed? You don't know me."

He was right about that. At least I didn't know him anymore. "Maybe I don't," I said, "but I don't think you know you either. You're searching for something, and I hope you find what you're looking for." A few students came out of the girls' restroom and stared at me for a quick second.

"I'm not looking for anything," he said.

"But you're looking for somebody." His face transfigured. "Jayrin, do you remember those times you went to church with me?" He nodded. "And the one time you made the decision to give your heart to God?" Again, he nodded. "Did you mean it? I mean, really, really mean it?"

"I did, but that was a long time ago. A lot has changed since then."

"Like I said, you have changed."

He turned, and just like that, was a ghost in the wind. Didn't say bye or anything. I huffed.

I entered the office, ashamed to hand over the rumbled envelope. I extended my arm to the secretary. "Sorry, I wrinkled it."

"It's fine, Kamree." She didn't look at the envelope. "Are you familiar with the boy you were speaking to?"

"Jayrin? Yes, we went to elementary and middle school together."

"You know his mom?"

"Ms. Foster? Yes, she's a nice lady."

"What about his father? You ever meet him?"

"Oh, no. Jayrin doesn't know who his father is."

"Is that so?" she said.

That was weird.

On my way back to class, I saw Travathian. I had not said anything to him since I found out about the assault he committed. He had tried to talk to me a few times, but I ignored him. This time, he looked at me and continued walking to his destination without saying a word. And for some reason, a miserable taste in my gut overtook me.

My dad hadn't come home yet. He was still in Nashville. I talked to him on the phone a couple of times this week, but the conversations were quiet, staring contests. Neither one of us blinked our mouths much. Nothing much to say.

I anxiously waited for my mom to come home from work. She would usually arrive soon after I came home. I was in the kitchen, eating an after-school snack when the door chimed open. My mom came in with a bag of groceries and clanged her keys on the kitchen island.

"Hello, Aceson. How was your day?"

"Fine, I guess. Nothing special."

"Great, I guess. Hope it was a large, pretty bow to wrap up your week."

I gave her a side-eye. "Pretty bow, mom?"

"Okay, okay," she said in a half-hearted apology.

She began putting food away, so it was as good a time as any to bring it up.

"Well, there was this one kid who I met at school this week."

"Oh," she said, sounding surprised. "Somebody you just became familiar with? Even though school's been in for three months?"

"Yeah, he started last week, the week of my suspension."

"So, what about this kid? What's his name?"

"Izaiah, with a z."

"Are you two friends?"

"Well, see, here's the thing. He did want to be my friend, but I was being all stupid and told him I couldn't be his friend."

She handed me a couple of cans of soup to put in the cupboard.

"Oh, honey, why would you do that? Is he a bad kid or something?"

"No, he's Black." The next sound I heard scared the bejesus out of me. A shattering bang hit the floor, and red sauce plopped and landed on mom's pants. Her expression mirrored the scary movie face.

She stuttered. "You said he's Black? That's why you told him you couldn't be his friend?" I lowered my head in a regretful bow. "Aceson, why would you?"

"I'm not sure, but I had no idea what to say. I have never had a Black friend before." Of course, she knew I literally had no friends before. "I wouldn't know how to be friends with him. If I had White friends, at least I'd be sure we had something in common. I don't understand what Black guys like to do. I've never been around them before." She slowly shook her head. "I know it's horrible. I'm horrible."

"No, honey, you're not." She grabbed a handful of paper towels. "What you did is understandable. You didn't know any better. But hopefully, you do understand now that you can't do things like that. You shouldn't base your relationships on skin color."

She knelt and wiped up spaghetti sauce.

"I did apologize, and I told him I would be his friend, but he didn't want to be friends anymore."

"You probably hurt his feelings. Or he could have just brushed it off. It's probably hard for him to forgive you for saying what you said. I hope he can, but you need to understand how your words impacted him. Black people have been overlooked and mistreated for so long in this country. What you did, what you said, probably stung him and made him feel undervalued, made him feel like he doesn't matter. Like he's a nobody."

Like he didn't exist. Like he was invisible.

I headed upstairs to my room. Honestly, my mom didn't make me feel any better. I still felt horrible, but at least I had a clearer understanding of what I had done and how Izaiah might have taken my words. I sat in my room just thinking about it.

Later mom called me down for dinner. She urgently sat my plate on the dining room table. She had changed from her work clothes and was wearing her black yoga pants, a white sweatshirt, and a grey St. Louis Blues hat with her hair in a ponytail.

"Mom, where are you going?"

"Um, to Pilates."

"On a Friday?" She usually went to yoga on Tuesdays and Pilates on Thursdays. "Didn't you go last night?"

"Yes, and yes," she said while slamming my glass down. A little bit of juice escaped the glass and plopped on the island countertop. "I'll be back in a few hours."

I slurped a few strings of spaghetti.

And she left.

I thought about what Officer Johnson had said: *jail or grave.* I was either going to be in a cell or in hell? Of course, I didn't want to experience either of those dreadful fates. I also thought about what Kamree had said to me at school. Part of me agreed with everything she said, but the other part of me enjoyed the money I made and definitely relished having a girl like Lexiah. I planned to take her to the mall—actually, Dymond was taking us—to buy her some clothes and stuff.

I had made more than enough money to pay back what those jack boys had stolen from me, so I could stop selling, but if I would be buying clothes for me and Lexiah, I needed to keep hitting the bricks every night.

Dymond and I left school again to hit the block. I felt like running from school had gotten better for me. I still wasn't able to keep up with Dymond, but I could get to Monae's house without being completely out of breath.

"You getting better, lil homie."

"Yeah, pretty soon, I'm going to have to race you at the school track."

"Don't get it twisted. I will always be able to dust you in running." I chuckled. "Plus, you still wearing a backpack. But I notice you been wearing a new one. That one's kinda fresh. But I don't understand why you always wearing one."

"For my books." Dymond shook his head. "Don't you have books for your first three classes?"

"That's the difference between me and you. Something in you wants to get your education. You'd rather be book smart than street smart. Me, I'm about these streets."

"So why do you go to the school every morning?"

"Nigga, I got customers up there. Students, teachers. It's about making money. That's why I go every day."

My mouth opened upon learning this information. There were kids at our school and even teachers who were buying drugs from Dymond?

****

Later that night, I perched on the porch and peeped the brightness of a full moon shining down, brightening the usually dark block. The cold air bit my hands.

"So, you still not gonna let me drive tomorrow?"

"Are you gonna steal the car?"

"I mean, I can."

"Well, if you do, you don't have to ask me if you can drive. But fool, you ain't never drove before, so ain't no way I'm getting in a car with you driving."

"Yeah, low-key, I would be kinda scared and wouldn't want to be in the car with me driving either." I thought that was funny. Dymond displayed a blank face. "It's cool, we can ride with you. It'll be like you're my chauffeur."

Crickets.

I guess he didn't have a sense of humor.

The night crawled by. Not many customers stopped to buy. Maybe the bone-chilling temperature was to blame.

Surprisingly, Dymond treated me differently and let me sell to most of the pot heads who weren't regular customers. He told me I needed the money more than he did, so for every four unidentified cars which stopped, he let me get three. I didn't know what to make of his sudden kindness, but I wasn't going to complain about it.

A dark Mercedes Benz with tinted windows crept up the street and blinked its flashing eyes. Another car for me and my excitement level skyrocketed to stand close to a clean Benz. I hopped off the steps and stopped at the curb to look both ways. Never take anything for granted. Halfway into the street, the vroom of the engine startled me. Was this vehicle about to take off?

I stopped for a second in the middle of the street. Nothing developed. I took three careful steps. Then out of nowhere, the Benz burned rubber, and I froze. I couldn't decide whether to run back from where I came from or jump toward the opposite curb.

My mind couldn't analyze the situation quickly enough. I'd heard that right before you die you see your life flash before your eyes. I didn't see my life. I saw the bright headlights of a dark foreign sedan. Pain immediately impacted my body's whole front side as it dropped to the concrete with a thump. A piercing screech ruptured my ears. My torso absorbed rolling tires, flattening my flesh and cracking my bones.

Air escaped my being. My spirit escaped my soul.

And my life became dark.

CHAPTER 38 ~ Kamree

My phone continued blowing up from all the posts. Though the volume remained off, the vibration purposely interrupted my sleep. I figured some pointless fight at a club got out of hand, and of course, some ghetto body pushed record on their phone and posted a stupid video on every social media outlet known to humanity. No interest in having my sleep broken because fools can't control their tempers. I'm so sick of the absurdity. My instincts advised me to turn the phone off.

But of course, I didn't.

Every time I drifted back to sleep, the buzzing jerked me up like a fly whizzing by my ear. I swiped at the air and realized my efforts were futile—no identified or unidentified flying objects were flying around my ear. I hate it when flies buzz in my ear.

I finally got to the point where I couldn't take anymore. I reluctantly grabbed my iPhone, thumbed the button to unlock it with Touch ID, and opened Instagram thinking I would witness some form of violence on Reels. My eyes took their slow time adjusting from the blurriness, and nothing on the screen jumped out at me. I opened Snapchat and still found nothing alarming.

While putting the phone down, my eyes caught an alert on the screen—a teaser from the STL Today, the city's biggest online newspaper: "Teen Victim of Hit and Run in South St. Louis" read the headline. I froze for a brief moment with my stomach churning and opened the story.

After reading, my knowledge of the event didn't satisfy my thoughts. The newspaper had not announced the victim's name, and the story didn't reveal if the teen was okay or not. I gasped and experienced a racing heartbeat with mental torments shooting through my mind, wondering who the victim could have been.

I couldn't sleep, not knowing where my mom might have been. I called her cell, but she never answered. She didn't respond to my texts either. I waited impatiently in the family room, watching television and snacking on popcorn and soda.

Finally, close to midnight, she came inside. "Hey, mom. Where you been for so long?" She walked right past me.

"I told you, Pilates," she yelled from the kitchen, the sight of our previous encounter many hours ago.

"Yeah, but it's like almost midnight." The refrigerator door closed.

"And?" The microwave opened and shut. A hum reverberated.

"And you never stay out this late for Pilates," I responded as I joined her in the kitchen.

"Well, can I go somewhere else and grab a bite to eat or something to drink?"

"But you didn't answer my call or my texts."

"I'm the grownup here. No need for me to answer to you for anything."

"But I was worried something had happened to you."

She stood still for a brief second. Her eyes were a bit red. "Well, I'm fine. Sorry, I had you worried, but I'm a big girl, and I can handle myself." Beeping resounded, and my mom opened the microwave and stuck her hand inside. Out came a smoke-filled bowl bursting with peppery aroma. "Thank you for staying up, but you can go up to bed now."

I put my bowl in the sink and walked upstairs to my room.

Again, unable to sleep, a crazy thought arose in my mind. I thought about all the fights my parents engaged in over the past few weeks. And tonight, my mom lied about her whereabouts. She said she stopped and got something to eat? Why is she warming something up in the microwave? My dad wasn't home from being out of town yet. Mom must have gone to see another man. She's having an affair. Oh, my goodness.

I know my dad didn't play the role of a great father, and I assume his duties as a husband lacked as well. He spent so much time at work, and when at home, it was like he wasn't. But to think my mother would cheat on him was crazy.

Or was it?

CHAPTER 40 ~ Jayrin

Grim darkness painted my mind and eyes. I sat up, wondering where I was, where I had been, where I was going. I appeared on the front lawn near the entrance of my house. Two men with long, dark wool coats walked past me and up the steps—obviously law enforcement. The men had undoubtedly come to my place to arrest me for drug dealing. There was nowhere for me to run. I guess my run had come to an end. I had to take my medicine. I should have stopped before I got in too deep.

Still sitting in my scruffy front yard, my hand found my pockets to hunt for the weed and the gun. But they weren't there. Did I drop them? Did they fall out when I got smashed by that car? My hands started prodding the ground, hoping I would find the items. Nothing. I needed to go back to the spot to retrieve them, but it might have been too late. They had me. The handcuffs would soon clink on my wrists. I guess I had to take this like a man.

Or did I?

My mom told me numerous times to replace the burned-out light bulb on the porch, just like the one in the hallway. It was a good thing I didn't because apparently, the two men didn't see me when they walked past. The shorter, White one put his finger on the doorbell. The Black one roamed his eyes back at the street. He still didn't see me. This was baffling.

As if I were camouflaged in the dead grass. Perhaps it would have been best if I took off before they realized I was hiding out.

But something didn't seem right.

Another ring.

The jangling of the chain lock echoed, and Mom opened the door.

"May I help you, gentleman?"

"Are you Ms. Foster?" the Black man asked.

"Yes, I am. Who are you?"

"I'm Detective Arthur Jackson. This is my partner, Detective Robert Glen." Both men flashed something, which I assumed to be their badges. I contemplated walking the other way. However, I wanted to hear what they had to say. I stood, expecting to experience pain from getting hit by that car, but I felt nothing. I inched closer to the steps.

"What is it, officers?" my mom asked.

The one named Jackson spoke: "Ms. Foster, I'm sorry to tell you, but there has been an accident."

"An accident?" My mom cocked her head in puzzlement. "What kind of accident?"

Jackson, the taller, thin Black man, turned toward the other man and then back to my mom. "Is Jayrin Foster your son, ma'am?"

I inched even closer.

"What happened to Jayrin? Where is he?" Mom's inquisitive words escalated into echoing howls. "Where's my baby?"

"I'm right here, mom. I'm okay. I'm okay." I made my way up the stairs. She clearly didn't hear me. And clearly didn't see me. Her eyes remained fixed on the two men.

"Jayrin was hit by a car tonight and unfortunately was pronounced deceased at the scene due to his injuries," Detective Jackson said.

I walked onto the porch and waved my arms frantically. "I didn't die. I'm right here. Momma, I'm not dead," I screamed at the top of my lungs.

She paid me no attention. She began choking out deep cries.

Her weeping warped into a screaming wail. This brought Jaiyce and Jaiyde running through the hall to the front door, stopping at our mom's waist.

"Mommy, what's the matter?" Jaiyde yelled.

Jaiyce's huge dark eyes darted past mom and examined the two detectives. He peeked in my direction, as well. Could *he* see me? Jaiyde clung to Mom's thighs, who ignored her, and Jaiyde began shedding uncontrollable tears for reasons she knew not. Jaiyce desperately pulled on Jaiyde's red and white pajama sleeve, trying to relieve our mom of her so she could continue speaking with the policemen or continue crying.

Realizing his efforts were ineffective, he slowly did an about-face and trudged back through the gloomy hallway. Mom relaxed and hugged my little sister.

"Jaiyce!" I hollered. He didn't budge or break stride.

A harrowing thought made me realize why no one noticed me on our dark porch, and it was not due to the absence of light.

After mom calmed Jaiyde, she invited the men into the house. I followed them inside without being detected. Once inside, she convinced Jaiyde to go to my and Jaiyce's room. Jaiyde struggled to oblige, but eventually, she burst down the dim hallway. Mom's eyes stayed glued down the corridor even after Jaiyde disappeared.

"Ma'am?" Mom stayed frozen.

"Ma'am!" Detective Jackson's booming voice woke my mom from her stupor. She turned.

"Yes. Oh, yes, I'm sorry. Please, come into the living room. I'll turn on a light."

They followed her. I followed them.

"No need to apologize, Ms. Foster," Detective Glen said as they made their way into the small room. "I understand how you must be feeling."

"Oh, really? So, you've had a child taken away from you, officer? You understand how I feel?"

Glen cleared his throat. "No, ma'am I don't understand how you feel; nonetheless, I know this has to be devastating. And there's no need for you to apologize for anything."

Mom sighed. "I'm sorry," she paused, "for snapping at you. Please, have a seat." Glen sat on our brown recliner, which looked like dead, peeling skin, and Jackson sat next to Mom on our black love seat, which was just as shabby. She breathed deeply and lowered her head. "So you say, a car hit my son, detectives?" She had calmed slightly. The men both nodded. "And how do you suspect it is my son?"

"We obtained his name and this address from the temporary driver's permit we found in his shoe," Detective Jackson said.

Mom quickly craned her head toward Jackson. "Driver's permit? My son doesn't have a driver's permit."

"He carried one on his person," Jackson said. He shot a glance at his colleague, "We found it along with," he hesitated, "other discoveries."

"Let me guess. Drugs?" my mom asked.

The detectives glared at one another again. "Why, yes," Jackson started. "And we also found a handgun."

Oh, so that's where my gun and weed went. The cops took them.

"You were aware of his dealings, Ms. Foster?"

"I was. Well, pushing dope, yeah, but I had no clue about the gun. But I guess I shouldn't be surprised. Ever since he started spending time with that Dymond boy, things went downhill."

"You said Dymond, Ms. Foster? Do you happen to know Dymond's last name?" Glen asked.

"Sure. Stansberry. Dymond Stansberry. Brother of Dynastie and son of—"

"Devon Stansberry," Jackson interrupted. Glen turned to Jackson. "One of the biggest dealers this town has ever seen. Killed about seven, eight years ago. Leaving a club on the East Side, his car shot up on Interstate 40. Dead on the scene. Him and his bodyguard."

"So, family business. The sons took over, huh?" the White detective asked.

"Yep."

"And my boy got entangled with that family. I figured soon as he started hanging out with that boy, he would get in trouble. And now, he's dead."

I'm sorry, Mom. I'm sorry. I whispered, knowing if I shouted, it wouldn't have made a difference. It would have been a vain, muted shout because no one could hear me.

"Well, we are not sure Jayrin was killed at the hands of someone wrapped up in illegal activity," Jackson said.

"What do you mean?"

"This isn't the M.O. of drug dealers or gang bangers," Glen said.

"What do you mean? M.O.?"

Jackson explained, "Modus operandi. It doesn't fit the mode or method of operation street thugs usually employ."

Glen added, "They don't run over their victims. Guns are their weapon of choice."

"So, someone rolled over my son? Hit him and then ran him over? And then left? This wasn't an accident, was it? You two are homicide detectives, aren't you?"

My hand perused my ribs, searching for pain, but I still found none. I remembered the crushing agony immediately after the car rolled over me the second time, and I blacked out soon after.

"Well, there are indications this may have been an accident. But the circumstances are suspicious, so that's why the beat officers on the scene called for us, and now it's under investigation."

"But who could have done this?"

"Unfortunately, we don't have the answers right now, but we will do everything we can to find whoever did this and hopefully get questions answered," Jackson said.

"In the meantime, ma'am," Glen started, "we will need you to make arrangements so you can come down to the coroner's office to identify the body."

A long solemn silence ruled the room. Then another blast of heavy wailing erupted from my mom. I wanted to hug her to show her I was alright. But it wouldn't have mattered because I wasn't alright.

I was dead!

CHAPTER 41 ~ Kamree

****

Unable to sleep due to rushing thoughts circling in my mind, I jumped out of bed and did some research. I insisted I could somehow find out the teenager's name hit by the car on the Southside. News outlets didn't usually release teenage suspects' names, but releasing teenage victims' names was a different story.

I downloaded the app Police Blotter Scanner to hear the emergency situations going on in the area. I had the app on my phone before but deleted it because of its alluring addiction. I would listen obsessively, mainly to convince myself that living in St. Louis wasn't as bad as some made it seem. But instead, the news reinforced my already daunting ideas of my city with its overwhelming crime.

Frightful.

Depressing.

And I couldn't get enough of it.

The blotter became my drug of choice. So I did what anyone would do when they recognized they had a problem. I deleted the app from my phone.

Downloading it again, in the stillness of my room, my thumping heartbeat pounded in my head. I took a chance reloading the Police Blotter Scanner app and wondered if I could find material on the *Past Events* section concerning a young kid involved in a hit-and-run accident. Perhaps the cops were still on the scene and communicating with one another on their radios. Maybe I'd hear clues.

Static crackled from my phone. Calm voices intertwined with the nonstop static. House fires, shots fired, stabbings...I thirsted to listen to each announcement: police radio codes, emergency service response codes, street addresses, more numbers flashing through the phone than a measuring tape. I clicked on the *Past Events* tab, and I spotted what I sought; *"11:21 p.m., 4400 block of California, a hit-and-run in South St. Louis...."*

But the following words stabbed me in the gut... *"Teen boy killed."*

The revelation of the victim's condition was horrifying, but I still desperately waited on a name and hoped it wasn't the name I was thinking of. I knew that when you hung around trouble, more trouble would find you easily.

I opened the story and opted for the audio transcript. Sitting up in my bed, I hesitantly pushed play on the device. Not much information was given, and I didn't learn the victim's name. I opened Twitter and found the SLMPD page to see if the St. Louis Metropolitan Police Department had disclosed anything about the accident.

Many stories on the page, but near the top, an account of a hit-in-run on the South Side. Still generic with no names given, but I had a bad feeling. Jayrin lived two blocks from California Avenue, and I couldn't escape the notion that he was the one killed, but I hoped my instincts were wrong.

That's when a thought came to me. Snapchat! Too occupied with the official, professional social media outlets, I should have known the answer about who got killed in the street would come from the people with their ears planted on the streets.

The best amateur journalists, who quickly reached a crowd of customers at the click of a button, proved to be the most effective way to find out the hood's happenings. And when I hovered over the button, I pushed it and learned exactly what I didn't want to find out.

CHAPTER 42 ~ Aceson

I was in my room sometime after midnight. My dad still had not arrived home yet. Mom said he was a penny-pincher. He would rather drive than fly and would instead get home late at night rather than pay for another night in a hotel room. Mom told me Dad would probably be home around one in the morning.

I slept very little, but I began drifting just as I heard the muffled shouting. Who was mom yelling at? Then a man's voice reverberated. Could that have been my dad? Or was it...

I perched on my usual step and strained my ear to hear. It was indeed my dad. Because Mom and Dad were in their room and not in the kitchen, it was impossible to decipher what this argument was about. But this verbal fisticuff did not lack intensity. I gave up on trying to figure out what they said and put my head in my hands.

Did Dad find out about another man? Did *Dad* meet another woman while out of town? This thing was spinning out of control—like my spinning head. Not knowing what was going on was killing me. I had to find out.

I stomped toward their bedroom, knowing they wouldn't sense me there because of their uncontrolled rage. The door was closed but probably not locked. To barge in would be the death of me, so I knocked with a fist full of fury.

"What do you want?" my dad yelled as he yanked the door open. My heart jumped out of my chest, and my eyes enlarged. My dad had never yelled at me like that before. He never cared enough. His indignation transferred from my mom to me. My mouth propped open, noticing red veins popping out of his eyes. But I couldn't let his demeanor deter me from finding out why they were fussing.

"What's going on?" I asked.

He turned up his nose at me. "What do you mean?"

"Honey, what's the matter?" my mom half-whispered. I didn't know if she referred to my dad or me. I waited for him to respond.

He didn't say anything, so I let out my own frustration. "I don't understand why you guys have been arguing so much lately. Like, what's happening to you two? Are you getting a divorce or something? If you are, just do it already. I'm tired of all the fighting."

The silence surprised me. I expected one or both of them to yell back at me for yelling at them. But they stared with pursed lips. They turned their eyes from me to each other. I swallowed, preparing myself for an onslaught of discipline— still, nothing.

I sighed and turned as I trudged back up the steps and to my room. I sat on my bed for fifteen minutes without hearing so much as a peep from downstairs.

I laid down, closed my eyes as tight as I could, and wished to God I could disappear because I was tired of my life.

The detectives asked if my mom could find someone to be with Jaiyce and Jaiyde while she went to the medical examiner's office to identify the body.

To identify me.

She called my grandmother, who I hadn't seen in about a year. I didn't know why, but my grandmother didn't seem to like me or my mom. She seemed to like the twins, though. Sent them birthday and Christmas money all the time. She said I was too old to receive cash presents, although she never sent me money when I was younger either. I didn't understand it.

I stood in Mom's bedroom while she sat on her bed and spoke to my grandmother. I must admit it felt creepy, like eavesdropping on her conversation. Honestly, though, I didn't want to leave her sight. She was grieving and had no one to lean on for comfort. The twins were too young. Grandmother never showed care and concern towards Mom as far as I could tell, and Mom worked so much, she had little time for friends.

"Hello, Mother," my mom started. "I'm sorry for calling you at this time, but I have some bad news." She paused. "Well, Jayrin died in an accident. No, he wasn't driving. He was..." her words trailed. I could see a film of wetness in my mom's big, brown eyes. "I need to go downtown to identify his body." Mom squeezed her eyes tight and tears escaped streaming down her cheek. "Well, I'm asking if you could please come over and watch the twins."

A considerable amount of time elapsed without Mom saying anything. The strain on her face grew. "Why do you always bring that up, Mother? That has nothing to do with what's going on now. All I'm asking is you do me a favor and take care of your grandchildren for a few hours." The anguish from her voice made me want to cry. However, for some reason, I couldn't.

Anger fueled through my mom's voice. "Well, if you can't, I'll just take them down there with me. I'm sure—" she stopped.

She sighed.

"Well, the officers are waiting outside in their car now. So, the sooner you can arrive, the better." My mom released a long-drawn breath. "Thank you, Mother. I'll see you in about thirty minutes."

Mom gripped her phone tightly while shaking it uncontrollably. "God, please help me," she whispered. "Please, help me!" Then a torrent of tears broke free from her eyes. I longed to hug her, to hold her. But nothing I could do would help her.

I guess God appeared to be her only source for help and comfort.

And just maybe my grandmother.

Part 3

Unreal Reality

"I thought I had a horrible life because I never met my father. Then I died, and I realized my life wasn't so bad after all."

~ Jayrin Foster

"But now I realize I couldn't miss something I didn't have. Unless I didn't know I had it in the first place."

~ Kamree Covington

"The news hit me like a ton of bricks. I didn't know whether I should have been hurt, pissed, or a combination of both. Or happy? No, that should not have made me happy. Not even a little bit."

~ Aceson Denner

Mom's visit to the medical examiner's office had to be hard on her. She was forced to behold my deceased body lying on a cold metal slab. She stayed strong for the most part. She offered a couple of whimpers but did not totally break down.

It was hard on me as well. I viewed my own dead stiff body lying there in the flesh. Eerie feeling to say the least. It was surreal. It was unreal.

Mom identified me. She recognized the birthmark on the back of my neck. She always called it my Florida because its shape resembled the sunshine state.

Back at home, my grandma was sleeping on the living room couch. Mom shook her awake. "Did the kids wake up?" she asked.

"No." My grandma yawned, then rubbed her eyes with the heels of her palms. "Well, Jaiyde is a sleeping rock, but Jaiyce, I don't think, ever went to sleep."

Mom started walking down the hallway. I followed. She opened Jaiyce's door, peeked in, and closed it. "Looks like he's asleep now," she said while returning to the living room.

My grandmother stretched her arms upwards. "I guess I should go home now."

"Mom, it's too late to be driving home. Sleep here tonight. You should leave in the morning." My grandma turned her nose up as she examined the bleakness of the room.

"No, I'd better get going. There's nowhere for me to sleep."

"You can sleep in my bed; I'll sleep in Jaiyde's room since she's knocked out in her brother's room."

"No, I don't—"

"Ma, I insist."

"Fine. Are you at least going to change the sheets?"

Stillness settled in the room. Mom chuckled slightly.

"Yes, I am. A clean set is in the closet. I'll get them now."

Mom walked to the closet, and of course, I did, too. No way I wanted to be left alone in a room with my grandmother, though she didn't know I was there. But she followed us to through the hallway. After fidgeting with items smushed inside the closet, Mom pulled out a non-matching set of a sheet, cover, pillowcase, and blanket. She held the items out to her mom, who barely looked at them. After an awkward moment, my grandmother slammed the closet door. "I'll be in the restroom washing up while you put those on."

My grandmother walked further down the hall and turned into the restroom while my mom stood frozen in thought. The slight slam of the bathroom door jolted her out of her trance, and she walked back toward the back of the home to her bedroom and began fitting the bed with the sheets. As she finished, Grandma walked into the bedroom wearing pajamas. "Wow," my mom said, "I didn't see that you brought pajamas with you. Did you expect to stay over all night?"

"No, they were under my sweats. When you called, I threw my sweatpants and sweatshirt over the pajamas."

"Well, let me get you a cup of tea. And, Ma, again, I can't thank you enough for coming over and watching the kids. It truly means a lot to me."

"No problem."

"Well, you say that, but it seemed like you were reluctant to come over at first. I was afraid you were going to keep holding your grudge and not come through."

"Grudge?"

"Yes, Mother. Grudge. For the longest time you have shown nothing but resentment toward the children and me. I wish you could have been more of a grandmother to your grandkids. Especially Jayrin."

"I love your kids."

"Are you serious? Wait, okay, I forgot your definition of love is a little different than mine."

"Yes, I showed a little tough love at times. Maybe I—"

"That's what you called it? You treated me like an adult when I was a kid and treated me like a kid when I became an adult. You tried to make my decisions for me. And you hardly ever gave me the time of day once I decided to keep Jayrin. You were not a part of any of my kids' lives. I had to fight and scrap to survive with no help from you."

"Well, I had to fight and scrap too. And I didn't just survive, I made something of myself."

"Okay, so I didn't finish school. That means I made nothing of myself?" Mom's arm trembled, and her eyes moistened. "You act like you haven't forgiven me for having my babies out of wedlock. But you had me as a teenager yourself, and you never got married. Why did you mistreat *me* because of my pregnancies?"

"Really? Do you not remember?" my grandmother snarled, "I took you in for a year after you had that boy."

"Yes, you let me live with you for six months and then demanded I get a job, which meant I had to quit school. And you allowed me to live with you for six months after I got a job. Thanks a lot," Mom said. "But ever since, you've treated me like nothing. Why, Mother? Why?"

My grandmother turned her back and began digging in her purse but said nothing. I wanted to hear her answer. Perhaps she was just a mean old lady. Or possibly there was a valid reason for treating us all like trash.

"You can't answer, can you?" My mom did an about-face and exited her bedroom. She walked to the kitchen.

My grandmother turned back to her daughter with a look of disgust. She followed my mom to the kitchen. I followed them both. My mom added water to a cup and shoved it in the microwave. "I don't know why I expected you to treat your grandchildren any differently than the way you treated me as a kid, but I was hoping you would."

"What are you talking about?"

"Mom, you never treated me, you know, like a real daughter. Growing up you made me feel like a robot. You treated me more like a business partner. Like our home was a company and you were the CEO. You told me everything I was to do, made all my decisions for me. And then when I started making my own decisions, granted, they weren't the best decisions, you basically fired me."

"I was only trying to teach you discipline. How to make it in this world."

"Why couldn't you just let me be a little girl? Let me be a teenager?" The microwave beeped. Mom gingerly removed the cup and placed a tea bag inside before slamming it on the table.

"Life isn't always like that. You have to be tough, rigid or this world will tear you apart."

"No, Mama, you tore me apart. And things went downhill, even more, when Jayrin was born. Why did you hate me so much? Why did you hate him so much?"

"What do you think?"

"I don't want to say what I think."

My grandmother turned her head, avoiding eye contact with my mother.

"Ma? You can't answer me?"

My grandmother turned back to her daughter, nose turned up, forehead wrinkled. She picked up her cup of tea from the kitchen table, took a deep sip and a deep breath. "The problem has never been you nor Jayrin for that matter."

"So, what was it? Were you that upset I got pregnant, again?"

"Well. It wasn't that you got pregnant. I mean, I don't understand how you got pregnant twice so early in your young life. Sent you to the best schools. I gave you everything needed. So why did you keep finding yourself in the same position?"

"What I needed was love from a mother and a father."

"I told you I loved you. And your father. Well, he wasn't much of a man. Couldn't stay around for some reason."

"I think I know the reason he didn't want to stay around."

My grandmother shot my mom an evil eye.

"So, what was the problem with me getting pregnant with Jayrin?" my mom continued.

"Well actually, it was *how* you got pregnant."

My mom tilted her head.

"You conceived after having a one-night stand with a White man!" my grandmother blasted. "There, I said it."

"Really? Would it be different if I had a one-night stand with, let's say, a Latino man? An Asian man? A Black man?"

"Karin, stop being ridiculous."

"Oh, I'm being ridiculous? You have to be kidding me."

As uncomfortable as it was taking in this bitter spat about how I was conceived, I couldn't pry myself away from the scene.

"No, I'm not kidding. I had a problem with you having a baby with a White man. There, I said it. I didn't like it then, and I don't like it now."

"But why? What does that have anything to do with anything?"

"It has everything to do with everything. You get knocked up by a White man. Married. Makes a lot of money? Yet, you are still living in this hell hole of a house, in this bad neighborhood, working two jobs, and just living the life," my grandmother said while swaying her arms like a game show host. "Hell, any Black man could keep you oppressed and poor, but you chose a White man? I just don't understand."

"Mother, you are so insensitive. I can't believe what I'm hearing from you." My mom left the table and went to the sink and turned on the water, which didn't drown out her next statements. "Who am I kidding? Of course, I can believe what I'm hearing from you. You are living in the past thinking races can't mix.

"You are the one living in the past, amplifying a stigma of slavery."

"What are you talking about? Your nonsense makes no sense."

Mom turned the water off. Apparently, she had turned the water on for no reason.

"You've never met your great grandmother. My

grandmother."

"Okay, I know that."

"You know who her father was?"

"Of course, I don't," my mom answered.

"Her mother's slave master." Grandma took a calm sip of her tea. She stood and made her way to the sink and poured it out. Mom walked in the opposite direction and sat at the table. "Yes, take time to think about that for a second," my grandmother continued.

Mom's eyes dropped. "I'm sorry that happened. But that has nothing to do with this. Just because that man is White doesn't mean he forced me to do anything."

"Karin, look, I'm sorry your boy died. But I am not sorry for the way I feel. You made a mistake."

"Yes, it was a mistake having sex with that married man, but Jayrin was not a mistake. Why did you have so much resentment for him? He didn't have a choice of who his father was. It was God's will that he be born."

"Oh, no. Don't bring God into this mess. I'm quite sure God's plan didn't involve you sleeping with a married White man in the back of his car like a little whore."

My mom curled up her lip. Hearing my grandmother anger my mom pained me to no end.

"Well, if I'm so jacked up and such a whore, maybe we should look to the person who raised me as the reason why."

Good comeback, Mom.

"I'm sorry, honey. You may be right. Jayrin was not a mistake. And his parents were not his choice. But you had a choice. You chose to sleep with that man. And you choose to keep that baby."

"Well, I wasn't having another abortion like you made me when I was seventeen. There was no way I was going through that again. I was not taking another life and have more blood on my hands."

"Well, you also had a choice to give the baby away for adoption. But you made the mistake of not following through with that choice. The poor boy was going to suffer enough problems trying to find himself, trying to fit in. Wondering about his identity. Being treated differently because of the way he looked. Your son had so much going against him from the beginning. Perhaps we should look at the person who raised *him* as the reason why."

Mom stood again. Her face tightened.

"And now he's no longer here. Maybe his blood is on your hands after all."

"You need to leave. I can't believe how upset you've made me on a day I needed comfort. Thanks for coming to my rescue last night. But you can let yourself out."

My mom stormed out of the kitchen. My grandmother dropped her cup in the sink just as the bathroom door almost came off its hinges from Mom's furious slam. My grandmother quietly grabbed her purse and strolled down the hall, stopping at Jaiyce's room and peeked in.

I followed her and stopped at the bathroom, wishing I could walk through the closed door to console my mom's grieving soul. Something obviously her mother could never do.

******

For some reason, I found myself drawn to the detectives, which would explain why I found myself on Monae's block with the detectives Jackson and Glen around one o'clock in the morning. I had nothing against police officers, but nothing about cops appealed to me either. My only real run-in with authorities was the policeman shining his flashlight in my face after Dymond ran from them. But I knew about the situations where police officers had killed unarmed Black men, women, and even children.

The stories were well-documented with a bright light shining on St. Louis. I remember my first exposure to protests, and riots, and looting. My mom made me watch television coverage and explained the anger people experienced because a grand jury acquitted a police officer after killing an unarmed Black man.

I remember teachers and counselors asking us if we needed to talk and process. Even though my mom tried schooling me on the situation, I didn't understand and didn't care much. Kamree, on the other hand, cried at school. She talked to the counselors. She didn't understand how I didn't understand how distraught she was. I told her she didn't know the boy. I asked her why she cared so much and why it mattered. She told me, "All Black lives matter, whether you know them or not."

I got older and started noticing the same thing happening over and over—Black person, usually a White cop. Cops didn't get in trouble. Black and White people marched and protested. Black and White people got angry. Stopped traffic in the streets. Black and White people destroyed buildings. They threw frozen water bottles at the police—blasted fireworks at cops. Black and White people got arrested. White killer cops did not.

Next door to Monae's house, the detectives knocked on the door. An older gentleman opened the door. "Hello, sir. We are sorry to disturb you at this hour. My name is Detective Arthur Jackson. This is my partner Detective Robert Glen."

"Leviticus Dobson," the gray-haired man said in a grungy voice, "and it's fine. I was up anyways." In the many days sitting at Monae's house, I had never seen this man before.

"Mr. Dobson, do you mind if we ask you a few questions?" Jackson asked.

"Sure, officers. Is this about the boy who got ran over?"

"It is," Jackson said, shooting a glance at his partner.

"Come on in." They walked inside, and I followed.

The house was full of old furniture pieces and hundreds of thousands of trinkets sitting on the coffee table, on the big, boxed television, on a brass shelf: snow globes, miniature birdhouses, porcelain animals, and junk I couldn't identify, along with a ton of pictures in frames.

"Thank you, Mr. Dobson," Detective Jackson said. "You have some interesting items in your home, sir. Do you live alone?"

"Call me Leviticus or Levi. My momma didn't name me Mister."

"O...kay, Mr. Leviticus—I mean Leviticus—Levi." Detective Jackson seemed a bit rattled.

"And, yes, I do live alone. The Missus passed three years ago. I've been living alone since then."

"I'm sorry to hear that, sir." The detective looked at the pictures hanging on the walls. "Children?" Jackson asked.

"Two boys. Both grown and gone. One lives on the east coast, working for a big company in Pennsylvania. The other lives here in the county. Maplewood. Works for the gas company."

"Sounds like they are doing quite well."

"Yes, they are. Very proud of my boys. Can I get you officers something to drink? Water? Coffee?"

"No, thanks," the detectives said in unison.

"Did you happen to see anything outside your home a couple of hours ago; around eleven o'clock?" Jackson asked.

"Yes, I did."

"What did you see?"

"What I see every night. Thugs out there pushing that poison to people."

"Did you see the accident?"

"Oh, that was no accident. That car hit that boy on purpose and then ran over his body. Then backed up over him."

"We can't speculate if it was on purpose or not," Jackson said. The other detective remained mostly quiet, just like when they were at my mom's house. "See anything else?"

"Well, it was dark. You know I've talked to the city a dozen times about getting those streetlights fixed. They setting those fancy lights up in other areas. Why can't they put some up over here?"

"I'm not sure, sir. That's the Street Department."

"Well, yeah, but it's also about safety. Ain't that y'alls department?"

"We will definitely make contact with them and see if we

can get something done quickly," Jackson said. "So you didn't see anything else?"

"Sure I did. I got these night vision binoculars I use for hunting." He pulled them from a bag and held them against his eyes for a short show-and-tell. "I can view almost anything, night or day."

"Did you happen to get a peek at the driver?" Glen finally chimed in.

"These are night vision binoculars, not see-through glasses." Glen and Jackson looked at each other, humping their shoulders. "The car was completely tinted. Except for the windshield, everything else was jet black."

"Anything else Mist—um, Leviticus? Did you observe anything else? Perhaps the type of car? Color?"

"Dark foreign car. I don't understand why folks insist on buying them vehicles from overseas. But they all look alike to me. Honda, BMW, Mercedes Benz, Volkswagen. American cars cost less and are sturdier than those foreign pastries. Now, the problem with—"

"I'm sorry, Levi, but what about a license plate number?" Glen interrupted. "Did you get a license number?"

"Of course, I got one. I put my binoculars on the car when it drove out of here." Mr. Leviticus pulled a small notebook from his plaid shirt's front pocket, sitting wrinkly under his blue jean overalls. He flipped the notebook a few pages, licked his fingers, and flipped again. "That fancy car had lights shining where the plates were, but I'll warn you, though. I only got a partial. That car got out of Dodge before I could record all the numbers."

Leviticus read off the plate numbers. "What about the

color of the car?"

"It was dark, maybe black or blue or possibly green."

"Anything else you can remember?"

The old man rubbed his cheeks while searching for information in his mind. "Yes, that other boy came out to check on the boy after the car took off. Then he ran back into that home a couple of houses down."

"Could you identify the other boy?"

"Sure, I could. He's over at the house every dern day."

"What do you know about that house?" Glen asked.

"The girl there gotta couple of kids, but she don't come out much. She gets in her car a couple of times a week. Leaves for a few hours. Don't hear or see much from her, but those boys they sit on that porch every day and night, and they do what they do."

I bowed my head in a surrendering act of guilt, wondering if people would remember me as nothing but a thug.

"Thank you so much for your assistance, Levi. This will help us with the investigation." Detective Jackson handed the man a card. "Please feel free to call me if you can think of anything else."

"Absolutely, Detective Jackson."

"Call me Arthur. My mom didn't name me Detective."

The short walk to Monae's house from Mr. Dobson's produced horrible thoughts about me. The old man had been keeping an eye on me the past several weeks without my knowledge, observing my every move while I was dealing weed to customers every day. There was a good chance he had witnessed those jack boys rob me too. But nothing to do about that now.

Walking behind the detectives, with each step, I imagined Mr. Dobson scrutinizing me even though I was aware he couldn't spot my invisible body. A heavy pound of disgrace, regret, and remorse blended together and sat massively on my shoulders. Was it worth it? Selling drugs for extra money, for money to buy stuff.

The day I observed Dymond hanging out by our school's side door turned out to be the day I sold myself for nothing. The day I asked the wrong question at the wrong time to the wrong person. The conversation took place a couple of months ago, which seemed like a lifetime ago.

✳✳✳✳✳✳✳✳✳

"What you looking at?" I didn't realize I had been staring. I snuck upstairs from the cafeteria to follow Dymond, curious as to why he was loitering by the door we weren't supposed to use.

"Well, I was just wondering—"

"Wondering what?"

"I mean, like, where are you going?"

"Why you worried about where I'm going?"

"Just wondering, I guess." I wanted to make a good

impression on him. "Where you get those shoes?" His eyes dropped to the floor. "Dang fam, why you all on me like that?

"I'm just saying. They dope."

"I ordered them. Now, why you asking all these questions?" His face tightened.

"I mean, you always so fresh, bro. I wanna be able to buy me some fresh gear like you."

"Nah, you don't wanna be like me."

"How do you know?"

"Trust me lil homie, you don't want this life. You ain't bout this life." He took his phone out of his back pocket and gave it a quick glance.

"I know what you do. And I want in. Why don't you put me on?"

He smacked his lips. "How you know what I do?"

"Man, come on. I ain't stupid. I hear stuff. I see stuff. I know stuff."

"Well, if you don't see it or hear it from me, don't believe it."

"Maybe you can show me. Maybe you can tell me how to do it." I didn't understand where I got the courage to speak to him with such confidence.

The jolting pitch of the bell froze me as Dymond shot through the door, leaving me standing wondering and wishing.

But with that short conversation, Dymond approached me a couple of days later. Said he would give me a shot. And it marked the beginning of my slow death.

****

Standing on the familiar steps, I thought about the stark contrast between the inside of Monae's house and its outside. If the detectives walked inside, they would certainly be suspicious of how her home appeared luxurious. Detective Jackson knocked on the door.

After a few minutes of knocks, Monae opened the door and appeared with her head wrapped in a yellow bandanna with some of her long hair hanging out. A long T-shirt and sweatpants completed her sleeping outfit. Her eyes looked tired. Her expression was even more tired. She was kind of cute, but short and skinny. Her skin was dark caramel, like my mom's.

"Hello," Detective Glen started and then stopped, "ma'am?" He looked confused. "Can we ask you a few questions?"

Monae hesitated, looked past the men like looking for someone down the street. "Knocking on my door as late as it is. You can ask, but I don't have to answer," she countered.

"I'm detective Robert Glen, and this is my partner, Detective Arthur Jackson. And your name is?" Monae tilted her head but said nothing.

"We would really appreciate it if you cooperated with us. We're just doing our jobs, trying to find out what happened out here. It's about the accident that occurred." Monae didn't move an inch or say a peep. "We were told the victim, Jayrin Foster, spent a lot of time at your home. This is your home, correct?"

Monae shook her head. "I have no idea who you're talking about."

"Also, a second boy was here last night. What can you tell us about Dymond Stansberry?"

"I have no knowledge of any boys at my house last night."

"Witnesses tells us they've seen Jayrin and this other kid

sitting on your porch, not only last night but pretty much every day."

Monae held her door open a crack, still not giving the detectives any information. I felt terrible for them. They were getting nowhere with her. She was a stoic statue—a silent snowflake. The wrinkles on their foreheads got more pronounced. Veins in their necks protruded. A deep breath of anguish escaped Jackson's mouth.

"Listen, it would be a lot better for all of us if you cooperated. You wouldn't want us to have to hand you a subpoena or a warrant to search your place."

"You have no reason to search my place. Anyone ever tell you that this Jayrin or whoever has been in my house?" They stayed silent. "Yeah, I thought not. Is there anything else?"

A part of me wanted Monae to just tell them the truth. After all, they were trying to figure out who killed me. But something told me that she didn't care.

"No, there's nothing else. For now, anyway. But we may come back. Hopefully, you'll be more cooperative."

The slam of the front door met the detectives with a howling thrust. I flinched as well. I didn't understand why I recoiled. If no one saw me, I was certain no one could hurt me.

That was probably the best thing about being invisible.

✱✱✱✱✱✱✱✱✱

I didn't want to go to school after discovering Jayrin had died. I cried all weekend. I had been afraid something terrible would happen, so I desperately tried to convince him to stop hanging out in the streets and selling drugs. He said he would stop, but he had lied to me, which severed our friendship. But I still wanted the best for him.

Prina tried to be there for me. She knew how I felt about Jayrin. It was strange how my thoughts about him changed overnight. At first, I only thought of him as a close friend. As my best male friend. As my only real male friend. Then I started feeling as though I really liked him.

Knowing him for so long, combined with having feelings of wanting a real boyfriend, basically made him the perfect candidate. Plus, he strayed from crazy or criminal activity, always a good person... until he wasn't.

After spending two days at home, my mom told me I had grieved long enough and needed to go back to school. How could she determine if I'd grieved long enough? Anyway, she didn't want me to fall behind in my schoolwork, and of course, I didn't either.

"I'm sorry about your friend." The voice startled me, and I turned around to determine where it came from.

"Oh, hello, Tra." I looked up from my sitting position on the front steps of our school. "Thanks!"

"We weren't cool, but I guess if he was a friend of yours, he must've been an alright dude,"

"Well, yeah, he was." At least he was for most of his life.

It was after school, and I was near the main entrance, a

place I'd sometimes read while waiting for Prina to make her rounds around the school, showing off her body to all the boys and seeking drama from all the girls.

Tra turned to walk out. I stopped him. "I honestly did like you. But you made it hard for me. When I learned what you did. I couldn't keep seeing you. You might not understand, but I have issues with people who, well, have issues. I detach myself from people who are involved in criminal activity. My background—"

"You never asked me, though. You assumed because somebody said something, it had to be true."

"But it was true, right?"

"Yes, but not the way you heard it. I did go to juvenile while awaiting a trial. But they let me out when the charges were dropped."

"Dropped? Why?"

"The girl whose nose I allegedly broke confessed to authorities what actually happened."

A strong breeze entered the building as someone opened the door to leave.

"So, what happened?"

"I broke up with her, and she came to my house throwing stuff at me. She began hitting me and pushing me, knowing I wouldn't do anything to her. Then she grabbed me. I tried pushing her off me by her shoulders, she fell backward and came running towards me. I put my hands up to shield her, and she ran her face into my hands and fell violently to the floor. To this day, I'm not sure if her nose broke from making contact with my hands or from the impact of her falling face-first on the wood floor."

The story sounded a little far-fetched, but I guessed he was telling the truth if the charges were indeed dropped. "Wow, I had no idea."

"Exactly! So whoever told you, didn't tell you the whole truth."

I dipped my head, seeing Tra's disappointment.

"Who told you anyway? Was it my cousin, Rodney?"

"No, it was a girl."

"Yeah, he probably told somebody who told somebody else, and by time it got to you, pieces were missing and probably some pieces were added."

He sat on the steps next to me.

"You broke up with me and wouldn't give me the time of day to explain. You're cool, but you always believe you're right about everything, and you don't let other thoughts or opinions sway you. That could be helpful in some situations, but in others, not so much."

Embarrassment hovered over me as more students exited the building. Tra's tongue-lashing made me want to crawl into a cocoon.

"I'm sorry, Tra," I said. "I reacted and didn't think there could be another side to the story. I have a hard time trusting men—boys—to do the right thing. The bad taste in my mouth about my father for making ridiculous decisions and choosing street life over me is hard to get over. I seem to take it out on everyone I meet by putting up a shield."

"That shield will block you from getting what you're looking for."

"Who said I'm looking for something?"

"We're all looking for something. Sometimes, we can't

see it even when it's right in front of our eyes. Tends to be invisible, maybe because we're scared to face its reality."

"Well, what are you looking for?"

"A second chance."

My head snapped slightly. "A second chance with me?"

"Everything ain't about you, Kam. No, I want a second chance with my life. I'm labeled as some thug, and I'm nothing like that. Just because I dress in drip, talk with some swag, people think I ain't about nothing. I got accused of something I didn't do, but it didn't matter. I fit the profile."

"So, you don't want a second chance with me?"

Tra dropped his head. "Right now, all I want is to get through the semester with excellent grades, finish school, and get a chance to go to an HBCU. But most of all, I want people to treat me humanely and not like an ex-con. Including you, Kamree. You should realize that not every Black male is a thug or a gangster or a drug dealer."

"I think I know that."

"Well, act like it."

"That's a hard task. It seems like all the ones I'm close to are doing things in the streets and dying or getting locked up."

"Is that true?"

I didn't need to think long. It took me less than a second to picture my stepfather, Miles. He was the most positive male figure I knew. He married my mother when I was seven. Introduced her to his church. Introduced us to a wholesome way of living. They had my little brother Trueth, and Miles took care of us all. He treated me like I was his very own daughter. And I must admit I loved him like my very own father. "No, not true."

"Well, if you can admit that, then, yes, I do want a second

chance with you."

I bit the skin from my lip. "So, you forgive me? Just like that?"

"Of course, I do. Why wouldn't I?"

"Because I was a total jerk to you?"

"There once was someone else who was a worse jerk than you. And I forgave her too." I assumed he meant his ex-girlfriend. "Holding a grudge won't do me or anyone else any good. Just useless energy being spent on something that can't change. The past is the past, and all we can do is change what we are doing right now."

"Man, you are a righteous dude. Kind of like Jayrin before..." my words dissipated.

"Speaking of Jayrin, his funeral is Friday afternoon, right."

I nodded.

"I suppose you will be going."

"Yes, of course."

"Do you mind if I go with you? Or would that be weird?"

"Well, it sounds like you're asking to take me on a date... to a funeral. So yes, that would be weird." I checked my phone for the time. Kaprina should have been here. "Plus, you didn't know him for real."

"But I know you. And I want to be there for you if you'd let me. I could be a shoulder you can cry on."

"Well, I'm sure Kaprina's shoulder will be there for me, but I guess having an extra shoulder couldn't hurt. But this will not be a date," I said emphatically.

"No, we're going as classmates." He hesitated. "And as friends?"

I nodded as Prina came prancing down the steps.

"Well, look at what I stumbled upon. Kamree and Travathian. Are my eyes deceiving me?"

"Girl, chill, we're just having a decent conversation."

"I bet. But don't pay me no mind. I can walk home alone."

"Well, I'm leaving. I'll talk to you later, Kam," Tra said.

"Bye, Tra." I watched my knight gallop away. And some of my pride galloped away too. He helped me realize I had something to do, and I had to do it soon. And it involved a drug dealer, an armed robber, and a lousy father, all wrapped in one.

Every Thursday night, my family had a devotional time at six-thirty. Well, maybe not every Thursday. Occasionally, something came up at the last minute, and we'd cancel and pick up the following week. My mom, my stepdad Miles, my brother Trueth, and I would discuss Bible verses and stories and show how they were relevant to our lives.

They usually revolved around how my brother and I were doing in school. But we tended to drift into other conversations too. Like our country's climate, our community, racism, and on occasion, relationships, aka, sex!

At nine years old, Trueth possessed an amount of maturity which surpassed his nine-year-old counterparts. But he definitely blushed when discussions ventured toward sex.

I was used to it. My mom had talked to me about sex since I was about Trueth's age, so these discussions didn't bother me. At first, it felt uncomfortable in front of my half-brother and stepfather, but I got used to it. And our openness about the subject made me realize I could come to my parents about anything.

I unashamedly announced to them I was a virgin, and I planned on staying one until I got married. They said God intended for us to get married, then have sex, and I believed it. Even if I didn't believe it, I'd still feel the same way. I've seen too many cases with girls my age getting pregnant, having baby daddies all over town, struggling to survive. I wanted no parts of that. I had goals.

And the only fool-proof way to not get pregnant before getting married was to not have sex. That is not to say girls who had babies young or before getting married couldn't still be successful in life. I know tons have. But if God would rather it be the other way, I would instead do it His way than try my own way.

Yes, plenty of people did it the right way and still had all kinds of problems because stuff happened, but I was willing to try whatever it took to do things right. That fueled my desire to bring up what I thought was a crucial issue I was dealing with. I actually said something before the devotion started. I didn't want the conversation to go in a different direction before I could say anything.

"I want to go see my father." Miles closed his Bible gingerly as if he didn't want to break the pages. All three faces turned toward me, staring like I was a ghost. My mom peeked at my stepfather; my stepfather put his eyes on my brother. Trueth stared straight ahead, looking at nothing in particular. He knew my father was in prison. He'd never met him. Never even seen a picture of him. It had been so long since I had seen him, I'd forgotten what he looked like. When my mom asked me if I wanted a picture of him, I gave her an emphatic no.

"Trueth—" my mom started.

"No, Toria, he should hear this," my stepfather said.

"But this has nothing to do with him."

"He's in this family, so this does have something to do with him. Besides, he's a boy. He needs to learn every side of fatherhood. He can handle this just like he can handle everything we throw at him." My mom didn't appear to be convinced but balked at commenting further.

"What brought this about, Kamree?" she asked.

"I think I need to see him. Talk to him. I'm still harboring unforgiveness toward him, and I think, no, I know it has affected the way I view all men." I hesitated. "But not you, Daddy." I stopped calling him Miles a long time ago. "Boys at school. Stuff on the news. I'm angry and full of distrust. I think it has a lot to do with my heart being hard toward my biological father."

My mom squirmed on our black fake leather couch. "I don't think that would be a good idea, sweetie. He doesn't care about you or your feelings. You should let bygones be bygones. No need to dig up old pains."

"But they're not old pains. These pains are still here."

"But I don't want you walking in that environment. Prison is not a pretty sight."

"Mom," I announced, somewhat annoyed.

"I think she should go, Toria." My mom and I both turned to my stepdad simultaneously. I believe she was just as shocked as I was.

"Wait. You think she should go?" Mom asked. "Why? You thought protecting her was as good a thing to do as I did. Why are you changing your mind now?"

"Because now's the time. She'll be sixteen soon. And soon, she'll be grown, off to college, and on her own, preparing for her future. Too many things will be going on, and if she feels this is the right time, then it's the right time."

"But I don't believe she can handle it."

"Toria, you and I both know she is mature beyond her age. She can handle almost anything. You, I mean, we did a great job with her. She got this."

I always knew my stepdad had faith in me, but it always felt good when he said it and showed it to me.

"But Miles, there's no telling what might come out of his

mouth."

"Exactly," he said.

"What does that mean?"

"We don't know. So, there is a chance he might tell her he's sorry. He may tell her he loved her."

Mom blasted a snickering smack. "No way in hell, he would say sorry, or he loved her."

"We owe him the opportunity to."

"We don't owe him jack!" Whoa! Mom went back to her pre-Christian days. Straight ghetto.

"You can't take away the fact that he is her father. There is a natural magnetic pull for a child to want her father. And don't kill the messenger. That's God's plan, not mine." Whenever my stepdad brought God into the equation, my mom usually got the point.

"So, it's God's plan for my daughter to visit her father in prison? I don't think so."

"Guys, please. This has turned from a family conversation to a one-on-one debate. Look, I get it. Mom, you're trying to protect me, and I thank you for that. And when Miles came into our lives, you and he vowed to always protect me. You love Miles, and you don't think for one minute he would agree to this if he didn't think this was the right thing to do. You do trust his judgment, don't you?"

"Of course, I do."

"Then, you should look at this like he is. Like I am. I'm not expecting to go in there and have a family reunion. Honestly, I want to do this for selfish reasons. I want to cleanse my soul of all the ill-will I possess for him. If he doesn't respond positively, then oh well. I can live with the fact that I tried."

Mom reluctantly sighed. "Well, I guess you're right. But, I think your stepdad should go in with you."

"Oh, no! That would be a big mistake. That man would explode if I walked up in there with Kamree."

"Well, I can't go inside a prison with that man."

"Oh, you haven't forgiven him either, Toria? You may need to go just as much as Kam needs to."

My mom sat frozen. Jaws locked in place. She turned toward me and nodded her head.

Frightening.

The only way to describe looking at your own body inside a casket.

Even scarier? Watching people walk by and look at your dead body; some cried, some held back tears, and some casually walked. It was as if I were lying in a glass casket, able to detect everyone's thoughts. I recognized some people in the half-filled church, but not everyone. A few people from school, including Principal Watkins, Dr. Meadows, the social worker, and Officer Nazarus Johnson from juvie.

Some distant relatives, whose names escaped me, were there. My mom's cousins and aunts and uncles. I often wondered if my grandmother made a point to her family to keep a distance from us. She didn't like us, so maybe she didn't want her family to like us either.

I hadn't been inside this church in months. The church my mom went to every Sunday and sometimes on Wednesdays. A small building with torn burgundy carpet, rows of pews with torn burgundy cushions, walls with peeling paint, also donned stained glass windows with holes in them. I never knew if the openings came from rocks or bullets, but it amazed me they never fixed them. The afternoon sun glared through the colorful windows' cracks, presenting a beautiful hue amid the tattered building.

The loud humming of an organ kept in step with the people as they continued in the procession of viewing my body. Kamree, for some reason, didn't come down to view my body. But Kaprina did. That dude, Tra, consoled Kam. Anger boiled up in me because Kamree didn't view my body and because Tra hugged up on her. No sight of Dymond or Lexiah.

It was finally time for Momma, Jaiyce, and Jaiyde to come down to the casket. Oh, and my grandmother. They all sat on the front row in the center aisle. A lady bent down, taking my mom's hand, trying desperately to usher her up from her seat. By that time, Mom had started crying. She appeared as though she wanted to rise, but a gravitational force kept pulling her down. The annoying organ music simmered to a soft, choppy whisper.

Then, while still focusing on my mother, a white speck appeared in the corner of my eye and moved toward me with a hurried pace. A White man I had never seen before. He strolled past my casket, peeped in at me, and kept moving without missing a beat. My eyes followed his figure as he walked past my mom. Her eyes glued tight to him, and she displayed a sour scowl as her neck turned to watch him walk out of the door.

The curiosity intrigued me. First, who was that man? And secondly, why did mom look at him like he stole something? I wanted to follow him, but I also wanted to be there when my family came to say their final goodbyes to me. But it was taking them forever. I didn't want the man to escape before I could find out where he was going.

I decided I couldn't wait any longer. I quickly caught up with the man outside and watched him get into a dark BMW as he drove off. Who was that man, and why was he at my funeral?

I had to find out, even if it killed me.

CHAPTER 50 ~ Jayrin

✳✳✳✳✳✳✳✳

I wasn't sure how I got there, but I suddenly stood on a flat driveway leading up to a brick house. For a crisp autumn day, the lawn seemed unseasonably lush. One large tree stood proudly near the walk-up full of orange maple leaves. The home was as beautiful as any I had ever seen in person. I walked toward the front door. Behind me, a screeching car arrived. I turned and saw my favorite two law enforcement officers.

How much of a coincidence was it for Detectives Glen and Jackson to show up at the same fancy house as I did? Of course, they walked past me, practically through me. They rang the doorbell, and a man opened the heavy wooden and glass door. And not just any man. The White man from my funeral. The one I had tried to follow. I must have somehow turned up at his home. Now the coincidence took a twist and turn that I could not have expected. What did they want with him?

"Mr. James Denner?"

"Yes, I'm James Denner. Who are you?"

"I'm Detective Robert Glen. This is my partner, Detective Arthur Jackson."

They both flashed their badges.

"What can I do for you?" the White man named Denner asked. He looked slightly agitated.

"We are following a lead about a deadly hit-and-run accident that occurred last week. Tell me," Jackson continued, "do you own a black Mercedes Benz?"

He drove a BMW. Why are they asking about a Mercedes? And what were they asking about a hit-and-run for? Were they talking about me?

"I don't understand. Why are you asking me about my car?"

"So, you do own a black Mercedes Benz?"

"I don't believe I want to answer any of your questions."

"We're asking for your cooperation, sir. The sooner you answer our questions, the sooner we can be on our way."

"Well, are you arresting me for something?"

"No, we're just asking questions, sir," Glen said.

"Then I'm not answering. And since you're not arresting me, I guess I don't need my lawyer either. Goodbye, gentleman."

The detectives tasted a face-full of a slammed door. Again.

****

Considering the criminal activity I had indulged in during my final months of life, I'm happy and surprised I didn't spend time in the back of a police car. But there I sat, in the back of a police detective unmarked car. I had to find out anything I could about this, Mr. Denner. Who was he? And why was he at my funeral? And the hit-and-run? I needed answers.

"What do you think?" Glen asked.

"I'm not sure, but we checked almost a dozen car owners that matched the possible color and type of the vehicle Leviticus Dobson gave us along with those partial plates. And this Denner character was the only one who didn't cooperate."

"You think that will be enough to get us a warrant from a judge?"

"I don't know. But if the city attorney won't give us one, we'll use our trump card?"

"What's that?"

"He lives in the county. His car is in the county. We can

try to request the district attorney in the county to issue us a warrant."

"Oh, that's smart," Glen said. "What's the saying? Two birds in the hand are better than one in the bush?"

Jackson shook his head. "It's actually a bird in the hand... never mind."

They think this Denner guy hit and killed me. But it wasn't his car that hit me. And, again, why was he at my funeral?

CHAPTER 51 ~ Jayrin

✱✱✱✱✱✱✱✱✱

Going back to Denner's house proved to be more exciting than the first trip. We weren't alone. In the unmarked car being flanked by a few cop cars and a deputy's sheriff, Jackson, Glen, and I blurred through traffic lights and stop signs. This ride-along served as a joyride for me.

Denner didn't strike me as one who wanted that smoke from the cops, so I didn't expect any fireworks. But whatever was bound to happen, I had a front-row seat. And no one would ever know I was there.

"James Denner!" Glen blared while simultaneously bashing on the door.

Moments later, the door flew open. "Detective Glen. What do you guys want now?" He glanced past the detectives and observed uniformed police walking up to his massive walkway. "What... what's this?"

"James, what's going on?"

A short, attractive lady with dark hair, a dark tan, yoga pants, and... wait. That was the secretary from my school. The one who was acting all flirty or crazy or something. The one who kept staring at me. What was she doing here?

The deputy sheriff in the brown uniform passed Glen a piece of paper. Glen handed it to Denner. "This is a warrant to search the premises, Mr. Denner, including the garage. You two," he pointed to two uniformed police officers, "go inside and search. Ma'am, you will need to come outside and stay with this officer." He pointed and waved her toward a female cop.

"But what's going on?" the lady asked. "James?"

Jackson asked the man, "Is this your wife, sir?"

"Yes."

"Ma'am, come outside so our men can search your home," Jackson demanded.

"But my son is in there," she said as a lady police officer took her arm and walked her down the walkway.

"Mr. Denner, you need to open the garage." The man hesitated, then slowly walked with the detectives toward the garage.

I was torn on staying back with the crazy secretary to see her deal or finding out what was happening in the garage. I decided to head to the garage.

Denner punched numbers into a device on the side of the garage. The door slowly rolled up. The man, the detectives, and I slowly rolled our eyes up, following the garage door's track. It came to a stop.

"There it is," Glen said, pointing at a dark Mercedes Benz. "License plate is a match, assuming this last digit is correct: seven. Alright, boys, let's get this one on the truck and take it to the lab."

Men in blue jumpsuits begin walking down the driveway toward the massive tow truck with the police shield painted on its doors.

Glen continued, "Look at that, a clean Benz and a BMW, both sitting pretty in the garage. It must be nice living the life out here in the suburbs."

"Mr. Denner," Jackson said, "where were you last Friday night around eleven o'clock?"

"Why? What is this about?"

"We have reason to believe this vehicle was involved in a hit-and-run death at that time. So, I'm going to ask you once more; where were you last Friday around eleven o'clock pm?"

The man froze.

"And if we find any evidence on that car tying to the victim, we will have what we need to arrest you."

"Hit and run. What hit-and-run?"

"Jayrin Foster. Fifteen-year-old boy."

Denner's eyes got large.

"I was out of town, well, on my way home. I guess I was here in St. Louis by that time. I... I don't know," he stammered. "But—"

He hesitated. He seemed to be thinking, making calculations.

"Wait." Another long pause. "You don't have to take the car to get checked out."

"Why is that, sir?" Glen asked.

The other detective stepped in. "Before you say anything else, I need to read you your Miranda rights." Jackson recited them.

The man, Denner, said, "Can I call my lawyer?"

Jackson nodded his head.

So, they were arresting this man for killing me, and he happened to come to my funeral. And he happened to be married to the crazy lady who happened to be a secretary at my school. My head was spinning, and I didn't know what to think.

He walked toward the house. "James, what is it?" his wife asked.

A boy walked onto the porch. "Mom, what's going on?" Denner walked past the boy. "Dad!" he cried out.

Moments later, Denner appeared, cell phone to his ear. He yelled out to the detectives. "Where am I going?"

"Downtown precinct."

He spoke again into the phone. Then he hugged his wife and the boy. They cried out to him, not wanting to let him go, but he broke free from their grip. "It's going to be okay," he said calmly. He walked to the officers, turned toward the porch while being handcuffed with his hands behind his back. His family, still unsure of what was happening, continued screaming out and crying. James turned away from them and trudged toward the detectives' car.

I sat in the back of the car with Denner. I had so many questions to ask him, but unfortunately, he wouldn't have heard me because, apparently, he had killed me.

✳✳✳✳✳✳✳✳✳

Beautiful downtown St. Louis. The once bright but chilly autumn day gave way to a dark, bitter night. The Gateway Arch, the six hundred and thirty-foot symbol of the city, shone with a slight luster and a blinking red dot like a traffic light in the sky. Many white lights from skyscrapers mimicked the scattered stars across the blackened sky.

James Denner's day resembled that cold Friday. It started with my funeral and ended with a trip to the newly built, high-tech police headquarters. He sat in the holding cell as quiet as a church mouse. I sat there as well, trying to figure him out. Wondering why in the world he had killed me.

What did I ever do to him? Did his wife tell him I looked at her funny? But she stared at me first. Was this some sick, twisted scheme for rich White people to exterminate poor Black boys? Were they rival drug dealers trying to eliminate the competition? No way, not from pushing a little weed. I didn't sell enough to hurt somebody or another dealer's business.

He could have been high when he hit me. After all, he most likely came down there to buy something. He could have been a pothead.

I had a feeling he would not say anything to help solve this mystery. He sat miserably still on a bed that resembled a floating mat against the wall. I stood to his right, anxious about how the next several moments would unfold.

Keys rattled. "Your lawyer is here," a policeman said. The heavy metal door laboriously opened. An older White gentleman with slick dark hair and an expensive-looking suit entered.

"Sabastian. What the hell took you so long?"

"Happy to see you too. What did you get yourself into, James?"

They both swung their heads toward the door.

"Can I get a moment with my client?" the man asked the police officer. The officer left and turned the key, locking the three of us in the cell.

"A hit-and-run? Had you been drinking? Wait, don't answer that," the man interjected sharply.

"When can you get me out of here?" Denner asked.

"It's Friday. No judges are going to listen to your pleas to leave on a Friday night. More than likely, you'll be able to leave sometime Monday."

"Monday? You mean I have to stay in this rathole for the weekend?"

"Well, actually, as far as jails go, this one is pretty nice."

"Sabastian!"

"James. Friday after six. Judges are done. They may give you a break and allow a release on Saturday, but don't hold your breath. I'll call early tomorrow morning to see if we can post bail."

"I just want to go home and be with my family. And..." his words trailed, hesitant to continue.

"And what?"

"And then, I want to plead no contest."

"You what?" the man bellowed. "Are you crazy? I mean, even if you're guilty," he whispered after looking back at the door, "you have a right to fight. There's a chance you can beat this. You know how the game is played."

"I don't want to play any games. I want to leave here, see

my family, and deal with the consequences later."

"But James—"

"That's the way it's going to happen. No questions."

"Oh, crap, James." The lawyer took an exhausting breath. "Trista's here. She called me and insisted that I pick her up."

"She's here? Why didn't you tell me? Did you tell her anything?"

"No, you told me not to."

"Well, can I see her?"

Another deep breath. "I'll go find out." He turned and walked toward the door and twisted his head back around. "You're making a huge mistake, James. I have no idea why you're doing this, but you're making a mistake." He knocked heavily on the door. "Guard!"

Denner dropped his head in his hands and rubbed his wrinkled forehead continuously. Why did a small part of me feel sorry for this dude? I mean, he basically confessed to killing me. But there was something that I didn't understand. I couldn't put my finger on it, but it bugged me.

The door opened again. The guard appeared with the lawyer. "They are going to give you about twenty minutes to speak with Trista in the visitors' room." All three men walked out of the cell, and I followed.

The Denner man sat at a small table in the other room. The lawyer left. Then the school secretary lady appeared. "James. What's going on? They wouldn't tell me anything. Sebastian wouldn't even speak to me about it. What is this?" She sat at the table across from him. The guard stood at the door.

James peeked at the guard and put his hand over his

mouth. He muffled something.

"What did you say, James?"

He repeated his words, this time with his head up and his eyes on his wife.

"When did you find out?" he offered, barely above a whisper.

The lady scrunched up her face at the hidden question. "Find out what?"

"About the boy," in a slightly fiercer whisper. "When did you find out about the boy?"

She swallowed hard. Her head tilted. She said nothing.

"Trista, you know what I'm talking about. How did you know about him?"

She breathed heavily. "We were investigating him for truancy," she started quietly. "I acted as the contact person. Looked him up in the computer system to call his mother. And guess what I found in the non-resident parent section? A non-resident father. A name. Alex Denner."

His eyes dropped.

"Crazy coincidence, I thought. I tried to brush it off. But something kept nagging at me." She caught herself speaking a little too loudly and looked back at the policeman at the door. Then quieter, "Not even a week later, I noticed a piece of mail on the kitchen island. I didn't think much of it at first. The return address on the envelope was your business PO Box number. No big deal. Until I examined the addressee. K. Foster. And the address seemed familiar for some reason."

I moved closer to them as their whispers became softer.

"When I arrived at work, I logged on and searched for Jayrin Foster's info again and realized why the name and address appeared familiar. Karen Foster. You mailed something to Karen Foster. Why would you do that? I fixed my gaze on the boy's picture. Then I stared at that name on the screen. Alex Denner. Cute. You gave her part of your middle name as your first name. Very creative, James."

James Denner rested his face on his fist and sighed.

"That bastard was fifteen years old, James. Fifteen years ago, I suffered a miscarriage and a still-born birth, and you were out screwing some Black girl and getting her pregnant?"

Wait! I shook my head. Did I just hear what I had just heard? Is this James Denner guy or Alex or whatever his name is, my father? Are you freakin' kidding me?

"Trista, I'm sorry," he whispered. "I don't know what to say, except, I'm sorry."

"How did it happen, James? Why did it happen?" Her tone remained quiet but furious.

A long pause.

"I was at a bar, drinking, of course. A few college students came in. I had my eye on her. Offered to buy her a drink. We started talking, which led to one lust-filled colossal mistake. Afterward, I gave her my business phone number, and yes, a sort of fake name, thinking possibly we'd hook up again. But the next time she called me six weeks later, she told me she was pregnant. I freaked out. Told her I would provide money for an abortion. She vehemently opposed it."

He took a deep swallow, followed by a deeper breath.

He continued: "Later, she told me she decided to give the baby up for adoption. We agreed we would not pursue any type of relationship, count our losses, and call it quits." He bobbed his head up and down, up and down in the stillness of the quiet.

"The next time she called, I was furious because we were never to communicate again. But what she told me took me way past furious."

He paused. The lady said nothing. The guard at the door was halfway paying attention. I stood still invisible, in utter shock.

"She said she was keeping the baby. My insides boiled over. I cursed her out and told her I wanted nothing to do with her or the baby. But she made demands."

"What demands?"

"At the time, I had just started the business on the side. Not making much money, but I still worked at the financial firm, so we were doing okay. But she wanted money—child support. No way I could afford to have the State take money out of my check. It would have broken us, and—"

"And there would be paperwork?"

"Yes. So, I asked her if she would agree to a certain amount directly from me rather than go through the State and officially have me summoned to pay child support."

"The envelope. That's what was in the envelope. Money. You've been paying her for the past fifteen years?"

Oh, my God. This. Blew. My. Mind!

"It started off small, but after she had two more children, she contacted me again about how much she was struggling. The boy was six, seven, I believe. Our business started flourishing so much that I had quit the firm. Ace was born. Things were looking up. But I still couldn't afford for her to go to the State. So, I agreed to increase the amount."

"How much?"

"From three hundred a month to seven hundred fifty."

"Seven hundred and fifty dollars?"

"I researched. Based on how much money we brought home from the business, the State would have demanded eleven, twelve hundred easily."

And then maybe I wouldn't have been out there on the block trying to make extra money selling dope!

"That's why she had my name on his school records. It surely wasn't on the birth certificate, but if I'd ever stopped paying her, she could use those records to possibly show I was the father, force me to take a paternity test, and then force me to pay child support until he turned twenty-one."

Is that why he hit me and ran me over? Did he grow tired of paying my mother money each month? I wanted to scream, but instead, all three of us sat deathly quiet for what seemed like an eternity. Until James Denner viewed the guard's inattentiveness. Then Denner sliced through the silence.

"Why did you do it?" Another whispered covert question.

"Why did I do what?" the lady responded.

Denner gave her fierce eye contact. "Don't make me say it, Trista."

The lady caught on. She looked at the guard.

"Oh. Well, it was an accident. I swear." I could hardly detect her soft words. I moved even closer.

"Why were you even there?"

"I wanted to spy on him. Possibly catch a glimpse of Karin Foster." What did she want with my mother? "I drove to his home. Waited for one of them to come in or go out. Finally, the boy came jogging out and up the street. I carefully followed him about three or four blocks. He sat on steps with this other boy, and it soon became clear to me they were selling drugs."

The man's eyes closed tightly.

"I parked maybe one hundred yards back, taking in the action. All the cars had flashed their headlights, and the boys would run across the street to make apparent transactions. Then something came over me, and I crept up towards them. I boldly flashed my lights. I didn't know which of the boys would come over. I didn't detect a pattern. I took a chance, and the Jayrin boy came over. I freaked. I didn't rehearse what I would say. Before he stood in front of my car, I panicked, put the car in drive, and blasted off. I saw the terror in his eyes as he froze. I hit him and rolled over him. Then I backed up, in disbelief to what I had done."

I put my hand on my side again. Still no pain. But I remember that car rolling over me.

"Suddenly, the other kid ran towards me." I stood in silence and detected the terror in her eyes as she continued speaking softly. "I got frightened and drove off." It sounded like she was beginning to cry. "I tried my hardest not to roll over that boy again and drove around him, but I didn't stop, and I didn't look back. It was an accident. I promise I didn't mean to."

Her eyes tightened.

A long quiet moment stood still.

"Ten minutes!" the guard barked out. They both looked back.

"And why are you doing this?" she continued. "Do you feel guilty or something?"

He shook his head. Still whispering, "You know, sometimes we get to enjoy things we don't deserve, and sometimes we deserve punishment and are granted mercy instead. I messed up, Trista. But I'm not doing this just because I messed up. I'm doing this because, as your husband, I am supposed to sacrifice all for you. There's no way I will have my wife in prison for this horrible mistake."

"But I'm getting off on something I did."

"I hate to say this Tris, but you aren't getting off. I'm pretty sure you will have a lifetime of guilt.

"But, is it right? You lying about—"

"The only thing I'm confessing is that the car that's in my name hit the boy. And then I'm pleading no contest, which means I'm not confessing to actually doing it."

"But how will Ace and I make it financially without you?"

"There's plenty of money in our savings account and in the company's savings account. I will make sure Sebastian has money transferred to you each month, and pretty much all the bills are automatic withdrawals. You'll be fine."

Even though no one could see it, my mouth was wide open, in total shock.

James Denner, my father, didn't kill me. He was just taking the blame for it.

✳✳✳✳✳✳✳✳

Mom took a day off from her part-time job. After the funeral the day before, she undoubtedly needed a break. The weekend usually consisted of her working at the corner store Friday evening and most of the day on Saturday and then going to church Sunday. She didn't work at all Friday and slept in Saturday morning, and so did Jaiyce and Jaiyde. The house remained quiet and somber until a knock disturbed the peace.

My mom went to the door and peeked out. She double-checked and pulled her robe together in the front. Fluffed her hair a bit. She proceeded to unravel the security door chain, twisted the knob on the deadbolt lock, and gently opened the door. The detectives were standing before her.

"Detectives, how...what can I do for you?"

"Good morning Ms. Foster. Sorry to bother you so early. Hope we didn't wake you," Jackson said.

"Oh, no worries. It's, what, nine-fifteen, nine-twenty? I was just..." She was just lying in her bed, thinking about me, probably.

"Well, ma'am, we do need to report some news to you."

"More bad news? Although I don't believe my life can get any worse."

"I would say some bad news, and maybe some good news as well," Detective Jackson said.

"Come on in. Have a seat in the living room."

The two men walked inside and stopped. "If you don't mind, we'll just stay right here, ma'am. We don't have much time, and we'll need to leave shortly."

"Sure." She scanned them both. "Well, give me the bad

news first."

The gentlemen shared glances. Glen spoke: "We tested the gun we found on your son the night of the accident for ballistics. Turns out, the weapon was used in a murder."

A small yelp escaped my mom's mouth. A heavy anchor dropped in my stomach. Mom's voice remained soft, shaky, and unsure. "Are you saying Jayrin murdered somebody?"

Jackson took a quick breath. "There's reason to believe so."

Wait! What were they talking about? I never fired that gun. Never. "Does the name Erique Timmons mean anything to you? Did Jayrin ever bring up his name?"

"No, I've never heard of him?"

"Well, Erique Timmons was shot and killed several blocks east of here a little more than a few weeks ago. Killed with the weapon we found on Jayrin."

What? I didn't kill Erique. I didn't even have that gun when he got shot. Dymond gave it to me... my thoughts trailed off... the day after Erique was killed. We talked about the murder that night, and later he gave me the gun and the phones.

Did y'all check for fingerprints? I thundered, forgetting they couldn't hear me. Did you see somebody else's fingerprints on it? I then realized they would never find Dymond's fingerprints on the weapon. He always wore gloves, including the night he had handed me the pistol.

"I can't believe it. I figured things got bad, but I didn't think that they were to the point where he was killing folk."

But I didn't, Mom. I didn't kill that boy. I promise I didn't.

"So, what does this mean?"

"The case will go from a cold case to case closed."

My mom put her hands on top of her head, licked her lips, and said, "So I can't imagine there is some good news." Her voice quivered.

"Well, yes, we've arrested and charged a suspect concerning your son's hit-and-run death."

"Well, detective Jackson," my mom started, "I guess that is good news—sort of like picking up dog crap with a newspaper. Even the good news is ruined." She sighed. "Arresting somebody won't bring my son back."

"We understand this does little to bring you solace. But we wanted to make sure to deliver the news before it hits the media. Most likely tonight, including the suspect's name. Hopefully, by giving you this info now, it won't be as big a shock to your system later."

"Yeah, I guess you're right. Definitely slightly more comforting coming from you. What's the suspect's name?"

"James Denner."

Mom froze. The detectives sensed her pause.

"That name sound familiar to you, ma'am?"

"Not really. Well, the last name does. That's strange."

"Do you know someone with that last name?" Glen asked.

"I know—knew someone named Alex Denner. I haven't seen him in over fifteen years. Well, actually, I believe I saw him at my son's funeral yesterday."

Glen removed a small notepad from the inside pocket of his coat. He flipped through it, arriving at a page that stopped him dead in his tracks. He tapped Jackson on the shoulder and showed him the writing.

"What is it?" Mom asked.

"Ma'am, the suspect's full name is James Alexander Denner. I'm not sure if that's the same guy you know or knew, but if not, it's a hell of a coincidence."

Mom's hands immediately rushed to her eyes. A pitiful whimper wiggled out of her mouth. Then a burst of words swallowed the whimper. "Will this nightmare ever stop!" That was followed by a weeping wail, comforted by Detective Jackson's chest as she collapsed into his arms.

I wanted to tell her that James Alexander Denner was not the one who hit me. But, of course, I couldn't. So Mom would forever think that my own father killed me.

CHAPTER 54 ~ Aceson

Mom didn't tell me why Dad spent the night in jail, but the horrifying scene of him being hauled off in handcuffs replayed in my mind all night. Our relationship wasn't the best, but I didn't hate my father. I didn't want to see him like that. When Mom came home from visiting him, she still didn't say anything. She remained completely numb.

I felt like a kid on Christmas when I woke up, and she said Dad would be coming home soon. I couldn't eat breakfast. My stomach did somersaults. I sat at the large, picturesque window downstairs, waiting on him to arrive like I was a little puppy. I didn't understand why my feelings were so giddy, but the thought of losing my father outweighed all the resentment and ill-will I had been feeling lately.

A sleek black Tesla Model X roared into our driveway. Mr. Francis. The rapidly thudding of my heart skipped a couple of beats, just like on Christmas morning. My thoughts wanted me to meet him at the door, but I didn't want to crowd him. I had no idea what spending one night in a confined jail cell could do to a man.

"Mom, they're here!"

She was in the kitchen cleaning up the food I had messed around. She scampered into our living room, wiping her hands on a towel.

"They're here," I repeated.

She opened the door. I stood behind her. Dad crossed the threshold, and mom still held the towel in her hand, refusing to open her arms to greet him, so I opened mine, and Dad hesitantly wrapped himself in me. I couldn't remember the last time we had embraced each other.

"Thank you, Sabastian. Thanks for taking care of this."

"Sure, Trista. That's why you guys pay me the big bucks."

"So, what's next?" Mom asked.

"Don't worry about it. Just take a few days to relax and recharge. We can talk about the next steps in a couple of weeks. The courts will set a court date soon. Make sure to stay close by, and we will eventually work through this mess."

An awkward moment stole the show. Then Mr. Francis tried to regain footing. "Okay, then. I guess I'll be leaving and let you all," he hesitated, "enjoy this special day." He said it almost like a question.

My dad stretched out his arm. Mr. Francis did the same. "Thank you, Sebastian. I'll call you in a couple of days. I owe you big-time."

"Oh, I know. The bill is already in the mail."

Later that day, my parents called me down to the den. They spoke to me about the news I would probably hear later—that Dad was a suspect in the death of a Black kid named Jayrin, a boy who happened to be a student where my mom worked.

This confused me because I was sure Dad was still out of town at the time of the boy's death. I told them he must be innocent, but they refused to discuss it further. They did, tell me something else that ultimately left me devastated.

I sat in my room, paralyzed after the discussion. My dad had another son? Crazy. And even more crazy was the word *had*, meaning the boy had died. Not only did he die, but my father was also the one who had hit and killed him. This story was spinning like a top, and I felt dizzy and dazed thinking about it.

I had a brother. All the lonely nights of playing video games by myself. All the friendless years. All the days and nights at work or out of town, leading to an absent father who spent little time with me. All along existed a boy—my brother—who I could have played with, talked to, and fought with. But it never happened.

It got me thinking, though. Would I have been able to relate to him? Because, after all, he was Black. Well, at least half-Black.

And that was foreign to me, as foreign as speaking Swahili. I might learn the language, but I would stumble over it and fumble the entire time. The same clumsiness I displayed when talking to Izaiah at the lunch table. I didn't think I was a racist, but I didn't know how to react to having a Black brother.

That seemed, well, foreign.

✳✳✳✳✳✳✳✳✳

A putrid odor like urine mixed with sweat smacked me in the nostrils as soon as we entered. My ears couldn't fight back the riotous vibrations from the eight hundred inmates. The clinging of keys and clinking of metal doors had me jittery. I remembered what Miles had told me: "Take deep breaths and pray quick prayers."

The problem with deep breaths was inhaling the rancid residuals of nasty men. The problem with quick prayers was they weren't long enough. I tried to convince myself I hadn't made the biggest mistake of my life. My mom was with me for moral support, but her face indicated she needed moral support herself.

We made an appointment to visit my father five weeks earlier. They told us that after even making the hour and a half drive to Potosi Correctional Center, there was no guarantee we'd be able to visit with him. They said if anything happened that jeopardized safety and security, they wouldn't allow us to see our loved ones. I didn't believe that applied to my situation. I was visiting my father, not my loved one.

We arrived thirty minutes before our appointment, and almost two hours later, we still sat in the waiting area. My mom, who wasn't thrilled about this field trip in the first place, did a lot of squirming and heavy sighing. Her actions didn't help calm my jitters.

Mercifully, a female guard finally called for us. She led us to a small room where two male guards were posted. Our belongings had to be stored in a locker. The lady searched us.

Her hands explored just about every crevice on our bodies, even with our clothes on. I'd never felt so violated.

All three guards walked us to another room. Their hands held batons, and they made no attempt for small talk. It was intense. I had a burning desire to scratch my head because, well, it itched, but fear would not allow me to move my arms in any direction other than the back-and-forth sway of walking. I focused intently on my feet, not wanting to trip or slip or make any sudden moves, even accidentally.

After walking for what seemed like an hour, we arrived at a door that read *Fam ly Vi its.* I swallowed a lump and entered the room. A sour build-up filled my stomach. Inside the visiting room, a baby was howling, and a toddler jumped from an empty chair to the floor, barely landing on his feet.

A guard led us to that empty chair and invited one of us to sit down. I sat. One of the other guards scraped a chair across the floor and settled it behind us. My mother sat. We stared at a grimy Plexiglass structure for at least another hour.

Finally, a guard guided a handcuffed, bald man wearing an orange jumpsuit on the other side of the Plexiglass and shoved him down in a chair. His grimace caught eyes with my mom, and then he glared up at the officer, who was snapping one of his cuffs in a hook fixed to the counter. He reached up with his other hand and picked up the receiver of the phone. His eyes glared above me, and I followed them to the telephone receiver on our side of the glass.

I picked it up, but my mom snatched it from me. She stood. "Andre, this is your daughter." She slid back into her chair and held out the receiver for me to clutch it. I examined the earpiece. I frowned at the build-up of dirt and wax it contained. I reluctantly held it up to my ear, but not quite touching.

"Kamree. Look at you. All grown up."

"Hi," I didn't want to call him Dad or Daddy, but I didn't want to call him Andre either.

"What are you fifteen, sixteen?"

I took a quick swallow. "Fifteen." My voice uttered more squeaky than usual.

"So," he paused, "you wanted to see me?"

I hesitated. "Yes, I did."

"Why?"

My lips began cracking slightly. I licked them quickly.

"I," a rush of warmth waved over my entire body, "I was angry with you."

"And?"

"And being angry with you was eating me alive."

"So, what's this supposed to do?" His voice was intimidating.

My mom snatched the phone. "Andre! This is your daughter." She emphasized every syllable clearly and separately. "Can you act civilized for once?"

His demeanor didn't budge.

"I just wanted to see you. I haven't seen you since I was little. I wanted to let you know that I was angry because you left us. You left me."

He sat motionlessly. "Well, I didn't exactly leave you on my own. I wouldn't ever volunteer to be in here."

"Yeah, but you had a choice. And chose to do what you did. And because of that, you left us."

"Girl, you don't know what you talking about. You don't know what I was doing." He stopped and glanced at Mom. "I was just trying to provide for my family. For you. I did what I had to do."

"I didn't know much back then, but it seems you could have gotten a real job. Something that wasn't illegal." His eyes tore into mine. The receiver shook in my hand. "But I forgive you. I forgive you for leaving me. I forgive you for hurting us while you were out hurting others. I'm fortunate, though; I didn't have to grow up without a father even though my father was in prison. But so many other kids are not as fortunate. I'm sure you don't care about those kids. Why should you? You probably don't care about your own."

His demeanor remained unchanged.

"But I really hope you do care. I hope you love me. Because I assume you won't be in here forever. And when you do get out, my hope's desire is that you will commit to being my father again." My nervousness had seemed to have drifted away. "That you would do the right thing in society. I can assume it won't be easy, but I want to be there to help you if you let me. I want to love you if you'd let me. And more than anything, I want you to love me. I want you to think of me every day. I want every day that you are here to be a countdown to the day you get to see me again, hug me again."

A sniffle interrupted my chain of thought. I twisted my head to notice my mother wiping a tear streak from her face. I had delivered the speech I had rehearsed so many times the night before. But sitting there, I then began saying things I didn't plan to say. "I have to admit that my mother married a great man. That man has been taking care of Momma, my little brother, and me, and I love him. He's the only father I've known for almost ten years."

"I could care less about some other man claiming to be your father," he snapped.

I urged to tell him that it was *couldn't care less*, but it probably wouldn't have been a good idea.

"But I must also admit, I want nothing more than my father—the man who held me when I was born, the man who created me—to be in my life, for the rest of my life. Call me selfish, but why wouldn't I want two incredible, reliable men to help me navigate through this cold world? It can only make me better. But it can only happen if you decide you want to be better too!"

My misty eyes began to burn. Mom was sniffing like she had a cold. And I noticed a teardrop from my father's eye overlap the teardrop tattoo on his face.

Then he hung up the phone. He yelled, "Guard!"

The guard came, unlocked him from the hook, put the cuffs back on him, and they disappeared from the dirty Plexiglass.

CHAPTER 56 ~ Aceson

✱✱✱✱✱✱✱✱✱

My dad pleaded no contest to the charges of involuntary vehicular manslaughter and leaving the scene of an accident. He was sentenced to five years in a minimum-security prison, four of those for the manslaughter charge. Mr. Francis said he could serve less than half of his sentence and even fewer with good behavior. So, I hoped he'd be out in a couple of years.

I visited him a few times. It wasn't as bad as I thought it would be. Mom and I didn't speak to him through the glass, as I've seen on television. We were in a big room with other inmates and their family members. We sat next to him at a small table. The place looked nice, like a banquet hall or something. We weren't supposed to touch him or hug him, even though the guards let us hug him when we left.

Mom said I could visit him once each month until his release. The facility was a two-hour drive in Jefferson City, the capital of Missouri.

It's crazy, but I complained so much when my dad was at work because he didn't really spend time with me. However, since Dad had been locked up, I felt our relationship had gotten better. I wrote letters to him, and he wrote back. I checked the mailbox every week, looking for his letters.

Here's one of the letters I wrote to him:

January 10

Hi Dad,

I hope you are doing as well as possible. I can't wait to visit you at the end of the month. Being able to be with you right before Christmas was the best present ever. Sometimes just seeing and being with your loved ones is better than the presents they can give you.

You being away allowed me to recognize how much you mean to me and how much you love and care for Mom. Things haven't always been the best, but I hope and believe the best is yet to come. When I found out about Jayrin (my brother), I didn't know what to think. The news hit me like a ton of bricks. I didn't know whether I should have been hurt, pissed, or a combination of both. Or happy? No, that should not have made me happy. Not even a little bit. But it did make me reflect on my own life. It made me see who I was as a person. I realized that no one is perfect, and no one should be dejected or rejected because of who they are.

I had no friends because of who I was and how I treated people. But now, I have a friend—a friend who I previously rejected simply because of his skin color. I realized I made a mistake. Mom invited him and his family over for dinner for New Year's Eve since they are new to the area and don't have family here. I'm so happy Izaiah—that's his name—didn't hold it against me for long, and now we are best friends.

His life has been good for the most part, but it was hard for him to fit in because he was always different from others. He said it was like trying to fit a round peg in a square hole or something like that. He just stopped trying. He gave up.

But now we are friends because we accept each other for who we are. And we've realized round pegs and square holes can find ways to fit together, no matter what. When I thought we had nothing in common, I realize now that he's just a kid like me. And we can do things together despite our differences.

And I guess you know, Mom got me a new gaming system for Christmas, and Izaiah and I had lots of online gaming together before we went back to school after winter break.

I can't wait for you to meet him and his family.

Well, I'll talk to you soon.

Love,

Ace

CHAPTER 57 ~ Kamree

✳✳✳✳✳✳✳✳✳

My visit with my father was nerve-racking. Some crying, some silence, some harsh words. My father didn't say anything meaningful. I wasn't sure if I got through to him, but I had to remember I didn't visit him for his benefit, but mine.

I needed to be assured that I could forgive him, and if necessary, forget him. But I didn't want to forget him. I wanted him to be a part of my life. I wanted him to be reasonable and accept who I was—a teenage girl who wanted her daddy. Sure, I had someone—a stepfather filling that void—but to have my biological father there for me is what I truly desired. But the way the prison visit ended, I was sure that was not going to happen.

Weeks went by, and out of the blue, I received a letter from my father. The shock overwhelmed me. Ripping open the envelope, my hands shook from doubt as I wondered what it would say. And as I read, I sat flabbergasted. For some reason, he thought it would be acceptable to fill a letter to his fifteen-year-old daughter with over-grossing curse words. Oh well. In between the curse-laced phrases was another eye-opener; he apologized for his behavior when I visited and for the fact that he wasn't in my life over the past several years.

He did tell me he did write to me when I was younger, but apparently, those letters didn't make it to my hands. (I have a sneaky feeling my mother made sure I wouldn't receive them, partly because she couldn't stand the man and partly because she wanted to protect me from him.)

In his letter, he said he was proud of how I had grown up and said I had "balls" for talking to him the way I did. The letter had me in tears because he wrote that he loved me and always had, despite his numerous mistakes.

After reading his letter, I anxiously wrote back to him.

This was my letter:

February 22

Dear Daddy,

Thank you so much for writing me. I couldn't believe it. I thought you hated me based on your reaction when I came to visit you. But I noticed a teardrop on your face before I left. That gave me some hope that you cared, but I was still not sure. I hope we can keep writing to each other, and I hope Mom will let me visit you again. If that's what you want.

Even more, I hope you can watch me walk across my graduation stage in a couple of years. I hope you can walk me down the aisle and give me away to my husband. And I hope you will be able to hold your grandchild in your arms one day (a long, long time from now, lol—that means Laugh Out Loud). Basically, what I'm saying is I want you to be in my life for the rest of our lives together.

Before, I just dismissed you because I figured you didn't want to be a part of my life. But now I realize I couldn't miss something I didn't have. Unless I didn't know I had it in the first place. You were really never there, so I didn't miss you, but now hopefully, you'll be a part of my life, and I'll miss you terribly until you come home. And even though we can't get back all the years we missed out on together, we don't need to miss out on anymore.

Hope to see you soon and hear from you sooner.

Love,

Kamree (your daughter)

CHAPTER 58 ~ Jayrin

✱✱✱✱✱✱✱✱✱

Dear Jaiyce,

Taking an L ain't always about losses. Sometimes it's about learning lessons. If you ever wondered if you can learn a lesson too late, take it from me, you can. I'm living proof. Well, maybe not living, but I'm proof. Little bro, I know I left you and Jaiyde in the cold, but not for selfish reasons. Well, at least that's what I thought.

I figured if I started making some money, buying us stuff, get us out the hood, it would make life a little better for us all. I'm aware now that was a mistake. The most important thing was just to be a family and go through the struggles and successes together; instead, I tried to eliminate our struggles on my own.

You know, many pretty flowers grow in the ground, but some of them are weeds like dandelions. They burst with the bright color of a vibrant sun. And even though there are some benefits, in the end, they can cause damage to everything around them (I learned that in life science class). That's how I had been living the last few months of my life. Thinking I was making a sacrifice for my family. Getting nice clothes, buying stuff, but in the end, I was truly damaged. But I now realize that it's better to do the right thing than to do what you think is best.

I blamed not having a father for our struggles. But I didn't realize even though my father never wanted me, and though your father ain't there for you, it doesn't mean we couldn't have made it. I thought I had a horrible life because I never met my father. Then I died, and I realized my life wasn't so bad after all. When I looked at Jaiyde and noticed how happy-go-lucky she was, not concerned about our status, or anything, I wished I could've been that way, too.

I heard people say that their deceased loved ones were in heaven looking down on them. I don't know if that's true or not. I don't know if I'm looking down on you right now or not. What I know is that while you are alive, you need someone to be looking out for you. And I'm upset that won't be me.

Bro, if I were to leave you with one bit of advice, it would be to make sure you receive those people who come into your life to help you do the right thing. I was angry because I had no father, but I realize now I had opportunities to be impacted by people who weren't my father, but I rejected them—people like Officer Naz. To be honest, he seemed like a cool dude, and he probably could have helped me get out of the trouble I was in. I hope you never have to meet him, though.

I think about Kamree's stepfather. I think about the youth minister at Mom's church. Bro, if you have a good dude come into your life, don't kick him to the curb right away. He might be what you need. What you're looking for. I'm sorry, I won't be there for you. I saw the anger in your eyes, which reminded me of how I used to feel. I wish I could seize the bitterness from your eyes so you could see that even if you don't have a natural, biological father in your life, God still hasn't left you hanging.

Obviously, you will never read this letter because, well, I'm dead. In fact, even though I wrote it to you, I needed to write it for me. I needed to bare my soul and confess my faults. Perhaps you can learn this lesson from my mistakes. I may not have died by getting shot like too many Black boys and girls are, but I was still doing the wrong thing at the wrong time in the wrong place. Often, that equals death. Learn that dying ain't the worst thing that could happen to you, though, but dying without purpose or before fulfilling your purpose is the worst death.

Consequently, taking that death into eternity is an everlasting, never-ending death. But whenever you find yourself engulfed in the darkness of death, look up to the Son shining down on you. And by turning on the Light, you will be able to see the unseen.

Ya big bro,

Jayrin

P.S. Can you grab a ladder and change that lightbulb in the hallway for Mom? It's time our family no longer live in the dark.

EPIGRAPH

"I have come into the world as a light, so that no one who believes in me should stay in darkness."

John 12:46 NIV

"So, we fix our eyes not on what is seen but on what is unseen, since what is seen is temporary, but what is unseen is eternal."

2Corinthians 4:18 NIV

"The Son is the image of the invisible God, the firstborn over all creation."

Colossians 1:15 NIV

EPILOGUE

****

He had never hit one hundred and twenty before, but he headed in that direction. He had to. His pursuer was probably going about one hundred miles per hour. His heart pumped about 100 mph, too. To not get caught, he had to mash the gas pedal down. All the way down.

This was his first police chase. His adrenaline pumped heavily. He couldn't tell if it was due to the rush or the fear.

As he swerved in and out of the slowed traffic, he amazed himself at how well he maneuvered the curves, the cars, the trucks, and the pedestrians. He came to a screeching halt to avoid a vehicle in an intersection, and with that, he made a quick right turn—a half donut right in the middle of the intersection. The music blared from the speakers and sounded like a whisper compared to the roaring motor, the screaming siren, and his thumping heart.

He was oblivious to his location. But it wasn't essential to know where he was or where he was going. Besides, he didn't exactly have time to keep checking the Garmin GPS bobbing on the dash. It was necessary, however, that he elude the authorities and do it all in one piece. And alive.

So, for a second, he thought about stopping and surrendering. But something in his foot would not let up on the gas pedal. He didn't want to admit defeat. He didn't want to end the joy ride. So, it was full speed ahead as he dismissed the thought of giving up.

Houses and people, stores, and abandoned buildings, stop signs, and traffic lights. He blasted past them, all a blur as he floated on the streets, avenues, and boulevards. The sun made its appearance on that early Saturday morning but had not reached its peak. His eyes veered from the rearview mirror to the street ahead of him, to the speedometer. The morning sun pointed its rays straight through the windshield and into his eyes. He changed directions hastily, and the sun shifted behind him, chasing him like the police car.

He had one thing in his favor. He knew, eventually, the officer would most likely stop his pursuit. With the number of incidental crashes and fatalities from police pursuits that had occurred lately in St. Louis, the authorities would need to abide by their policies on car chases. Once the public was in imminent danger, the pursuing officers were trained to cease their hunt. He would drive long enough until the cop figured it was time to stop. He had to keep going until the Saturday morning shoppers infiltrated the roads.

Even though it seemed like an eternity, the chase had only lasted about fifteen minutes; he noticed as he looked on the dashboard and saw that it noted 9:20. Then he glanced at the gas gauge. Nearly empty. The vehicle must have been close to empty when he first got into the stolen car. His heart dropped to his stomach.

So, he began contemplating an exit plan if and when the car ran out of gas. He could jump out while the vehicle was still moving and hope the patrol car would ram into it. That would give him time to escape on foot. But the more he thought about it, it appeared to be an impossible option. A dangerous option. He would need to plot it out perfectly to allow him to jump out when the car wouldn't be going too fast with no oncoming traffic on the other side of the road.

Or he could...

Well, he couldn't think of another viable option. He hoped Officer Whoever would just give up.

He wondered why another police car had not joined in the chase. Maybe another one waited up ahead to cut him off. Then he thought about the possibility of him crashing head-on into a patrol car. That would be terrible. And possibly deadly.

And in his next deadly thought, he decided to stop. He began to come to his senses. He understood it was not worth losing his life. Giving up meant spending a few weeks locked up, and he'd be alive to jack more cars one day. The thought of death became a reality to him, so he slowed down as he ran another red light.

Then out of nowhere, he heard destructive, loud, mind-pounding metal strike the Accord as his arms quickly zipped off the steering wheel. A rushing punch struck his side as his body flew into the driver's side door. His head jerked outside the open window, and the momentum of the impact carried his body out as well. His foot got entangled inside the door where the window would be, and his head banged back into the door. His head clanged it like a hammer pounding a significant dent in the car.

The noise of two different sounding car horns and an ever-increasing siren shrieked simultaneously in his ear. Warm blood and hot sweat from his dangling head dripped down to his hands, which wimpishly dangled toward the glass-filled pavement. He couldn't move, although he had a fading thought of getting out of there and running as fast as possible. But he couldn't. His motionless body hung there like a crash test dummy, and he closed his eyes into eternal darkness.

When he opened his eyes, he whimpered in agony. His eyes blurred, and he couldn't see much of anything. After about thirty seconds, he regained focus slightly and caught a glimpse of a few people. They were talking to one another. He saw their mouths moving and their heads shaking, but he didn't hear what they were saying.

As he continually blinked his eyes while scanning the room, something came to him. The sudden sense of remembrance contributed to the discomfort he experienced in his side, his head, his legs, and his chest. The thought of a police chase flashed in his memory.

He thought he must be in trouble for jacking the car. But he understood that stealing a car was not a big deal when it came to juveniles. He would do about a month in juvie while they set a court date, decide on how much damage he caused, and hit him with restitution—a piece of cake.

As he reached to scratch his nose, he realized his arm could hardly move. *Oh no*, he thought, *am I paralyzed?* The sound of clanging metal proved otherwise. He realized that his arm was handcuffed to the bed. The sound of the handcuffs alerted the other people in the room to end their conversation and turn toward him.

He finally recognized that one of the people was a doctor; a white coat, thin-rimmed glasses, and a clipboard in his hands. Another person was a policeman; a light blue shirt, dark pants, a radio clipped to his shirt, and a belt holding a weapon. The third person walked toward the bed.

The man spoke. "You're woke."

The boy's lips were pasted shut with a thin tube stuck in his mouth. His sore throat was a concrete wall. He took a deep breath, which brought a resounding whimper and more intense excruciating pain to his side.

The doctor walked over. A short, stout man, his coat buttoned halfway up his torso, his round belly poked out like an out-of-shape bowling ball.

"I'm Dr. Stuart. You know, you are a lucky boy. You slammed yourself rather good. And to come out of it alive...well, let's just say you're lucky."

He gave the doctor a look as if saying, *What's wrong with me? Tell me. Am I dying here or something?*

Dr. Stuart picked up on his concern. "Well, this may sound worse than it actually is, but you have a punctured lung. It's called Pneumothorax. But I'm sure you don't want a crash course on medical terms. The condition developed when your rib was fractured. From the force of the collision."

The boy could feel a wave of heat flow over his body. Nervousness and fright once again gripped his being. A punctured lung didn't sound promising and left him wondering and petrified. He didn't really want to die, even if he always walked around like a tough guy. Being fifteen deemed to be tough, though. Especially in his neighborhood. Especially in his family. Swiping vehicles and trafficking drugs was his means of living, his way of surviving.

Ironically, the things he did were not helping him do much surviving. Case and point: being in a hospital with tubes through his nostrils did not equal the vision of surviving. It was more of an image of just hanging on.

"We took care of it, though. You'll experience some shortness of breath, but we pumped oxygen in you. You'll be tender for a while, but that pain will eventually go away. And you'll be back to your old self in a couple of months or so," the doctor said.

Dr. Stuart patted him on the leg as he walked away. The other man spoke.

"Dymond Stansberry, my name is Nazarus Johnson. Officer Naz. And I'm from Lewis City Juvenile Detention." His silver badge dangled from the lanyard around his neck.

The boy painfully spoke. "Lewis City?" he choked out. He knew the reputation of Lewis City. His older brother Dynastie spent four years there as a teen and often spoke about how hard it was. "For stealing a car and getting into a crash?"

Officer Naz looked back at the policeman standing at the door and then turned around slowly to Dymond. "Oh, you didn't just steal a car, son. And you didn't just get in an accident. The couple you hit is now in intensive care. And depending on their outcomes, you may find yourself in Lewis City until you turn eighteen and then going directly to the state penitentiary for a long, long time."

Dymond gasped with pain.

Stay tuned to follow Dymond's fate in an upcoming novel, *Snatch Away Your Name* by Jaer Armstead-Jones.